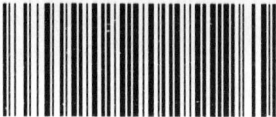

GW01459507

Romance of Chastisement.

This Facsimile Edition published by Delectus Books
London, England

Printed by Woolnough Ltd.,
Irthlingborough, Northamptonshire

Delectus Books
27 Old Gloucester Street
London WC1N 3XX

ISBN 1 897767 15 3

The Romance of Chastisement

or,

Revelations of School and Bedroom

by an Expert

INTRODUCTION

THE ROMANCE OF *Chastisement; or, Revelations of School and Bedroom* is the most exquisite, erudite and delicious of all Mid-Victorian literary works on the subject of Discipline, comprising an elegant collection of verse, prose and anecdotes on the subject of the Victorian gentleman's favourite vice— Flagellation. The writing is delicate, the poetry excellent, the entire volume as far removed from the (nearly contemporary) *Romance of Lust* as it is possible to be.

An earlier book bearing the same title, but with a different sub-heading *The Revelations of Miss Darcy*, was published by the notorious William Dugdale in 1866. The Victorian bibliographer Henry Spencr Ashbee noted "a marked similarity of style and treatment; several episodes in this volume so nearly resemble others in a work with an almost similar title, that there is reason to believe that both are from the same pen." He also stated that "the literary worth of this book is rather above average and in its way it is readable and even entertaining."

The later *Romance of Chastisement*, Ashbee informs us, was originally issued from Dublin in episodes by the author who printed 1,000 copies; and in July 1871 sold 200 sets to John Camden Hotten for £10, who then bound these sets up into a volume of 128 pages and issued them with a title page dated 1870 [sic]. A further edition appeared in 1888 from Edward Avery (c. 1850–1913), who inherited much of Hotten's flagellatory material after the latter's death in 1873. (N.B. Hotten's literary output was purchased by former employee Arthur Chatto from his widow for £25,000, thus forming the company Chatto & Windus.) It is from the Avery edition, along with the spurious title page bearing the imprint of the Tremont Co., Boston, dated 1876, that our facsimile is taken. The Frontispiece engraving (by Opie) is of Mary Wilson; the name of Miss Wilson, together that of her sister Betsy, appears as an author, translator and publisher throughout Victorian erotica. The name, taken from a notorious Regency harlot, was no doubt an in-joke among the eroticati of the time.

The Publisher's original advertisement for the book read:

> *The Romance of Chastisement. Only 250 copies privately printed for subscribers only. One volume, 184 pp., with ornamental initial letters. Post 8vo, vellum gilt, £2-10s. Rousseau has hinted in his Confessions, and the "Expert" has afforded fuller demonstration, that the "Magic Wand" in the hand of the pedagogue, mistress or guardian is more potent in its revelations, than it was said to be in the hands of Cornelius Agrippa, or Cinderella's Grandmother.*

The book veers towards the mystical. Ashbee comments: "Not only the administratix but even the recipient of the birchen chastisement feels a luxurious sensation. If the whipping is applied with a skilful hand, a kind of magnetism passes from the Priestess to the Victim, and she in turn becomes fascinated."

Avery ran his business and shop from a number of London addresses, chiefly 18 Carlise Street, Soho (1881-85), and later at 53 Greek Street (1888-1900), where a close eye was kept on him; he was prosecuted in October 1900 for selling indecent literature. He was known to have collaborated with other publishers of erotica, including H.S. Nicholls and Leonard Smithers, for whom he acted as main distributor.

In *Index Librorum Prohibitorum* Ashbee identifies the author as St. George H. Stock, formerly a Lieutenant in the 2nd or Queen's Royal Regiment. Stock also used the aliases "Expert", "Major Edgar Markham", and "Dr. Aliquis". His usual theme was flagellation and he never missed an opportunity to indulge his pet vice or to form connections with those who shared the same idiosyncrasy. Ashbee, to prove this point, transcribed a curious letter:

To the Rev. W. M. Cooper, M. A.,
July 17th 1870

Dear Sir,

I have derived much of both amusement and instruction from a perusal of your learned "History of the Rod"
    Being and having been for some years engaged on a work of a somewhat similar nature, it would afford me great pleasure to make your acquaintance on paper, supposing the wish to be reciprocated.
    Such a conjunction might perhaps be to our mutual advantage.
    To save trouble, however, I should state my view of the subject is tant soit peu libre, connecting it with Animal Magnetism. Therefore, if your sentiments be "strictly clerical" it would probably not suit you to continue the correspondence.
    Should you desire to do so, please copy the address overleaf.
    Faithfully yrs.

"Edgar Markham"

The author also sent Hotten further manuscripts of unpublished tales, which he planned to publish at a later date. He even issued a circular for his subscribers, but the book never appeared. However after Hotten's death it has been speculated that the manuscript passed, possibly via the mysterious William Lazenby, to Hartcupp in Brussels, who printed four of them in 1874, under the general title of *The Charm*, later published (c. 1890) as *Rosy Tales*.

It has often been suggested that the poet Algernon Swinburne, whom Hotten published at the time, was responsible for at least part of *The Romance of Chastisement*. It is undeniable that the style of the book in places strongly resembles his other flagellatory works, such as *The Flogging Block* ms. in The British Library. Hotten had earlier taken over the publication of his *Poems and Ballads* (1866) from another publisher who feared prosecution, and also published *A Song of Italy* (1867). Swinburne's obsession with flagellation is legendary and forms a common theme in much of his verse. It is common knowledge that he frequented London's flagellant brothels, chiefly in St. John's Wood, in the company of Monckton Milnes (author of *The Rodiad*) and others. A terse but accurate portrait of Swinburne is given by Gershon Legman in *The Horn Book* (1970): "One wonders what Beraldi would have thought of a man like Swinburne who, in spite of red hair, scrawny neck, short stature, a truly horrifying stammer and his unfortunate penchants for flagellomania, alliteration and falling into an all-too-bepissed epileptic fit in company, nevertheless wrote splendid poetry and some of the most magnificent invective prose (invariably on the wrong side of every question) in the annals of English literature".

The major piece of evidence for this is *The Whippingham Papers*, published anonymously by Edward Avery in 1888, which states: "A collection of contributions in prose and verse, chiefly by the author of *The Romance of Chastisement*" which, if we believe Ashbee, is the aforementioned Stock, although some items are credited to Etoniensis, a likely pseudonym for Swinburne, who fondly recalled his schooldays at Eton. A look at Swinburne's life reveals he spent many childhood summers at Bonchurch on the Isle of Wight, near the village of Whippingham. Whippingham Church, rebuilt in the 1850s for Prince Albert, was the parish church for Osborne, Queen Victoria's residence a few miles away.

The British Library copy of *The Whippingham Papers* bears the bookplate of T. J. Wise, one of the foremost contemporary authorities on Swinburne, and this would seem further to substantiate his authorship.

There is also evidence that Swinburne was involved in another Hotten project, *The Romance of the Rod*, as mentioned in the following letter from Swinburne to Charles Augustus Howell (February 6th, 1873):

Neither Hotten, nor for that matter any other man alive, has in his possession anything from my hand for which I need feel shame or serious regret or apprehension, even should it be exposed to public view; but without any such care for fear or shame, we may all agree that we shrink... from the notion that all our private papers, thrown off in moments of chaff, of Rabelaisian exchange, of burlesque correspondence between friends, who understand the fun, and have the watchword as it were under which a jest passes and circulates in the right quarter, should ever be liable to inspection of common or unfriendly eyes. I don't mean that Hotten could ever shew any such Rabelaisian effusions from my "festive" pen, as Rosellio or one or two others of his circle might. But I remember that when he was busied about his abortive book on flagellation, some sort of communication on the topic passed between us, and that I once gave him, what I think he never returned to me, a list drawn up in my hand of scenes in school which he was to get sketched for me on approval by a draughtsman of his acquaintance (I believe Carcoran, who did vignettes for one or two of his books), in which list, though there was nothing equivocal, or dirty in any way, I had the explained the postures for and actions of "swishing" to be shewn in detail, just as a boy at school would draw them for fun from the life, with due effect and relief given to the more important points of view during the transactions; and I would rather be sure that he might not shew it about for "cads" to comment on, or stick it in his blank book among papers relating to me. This is really all the matter, and I really don't know that it is worth all the ink I have spent on it. Of course, above all things, nothing must be said to Hotten which possibly suggest to him the idea that I am in any way apprehensive of his making it an instrument of annoyance to me; which in fact I am not, and have no reason to be. Indeed, I see he advertises a new Romance of the Road as in preparation, to which I should be happy to lend any assistance that I could, and so you might let him know, if we are to remain on terms.

The Anglo-Portuguese Howell was a fine draughtsman and produced many flagellant-themed drawings for Swinburne, for which he would exchange his birching poetry. There is also evidence to suggest that Howell occasionally played another rôle in Swinburne's life. In a letter from Randolph Hughes to Helen Rossetti Angeli, Hughes states "it is pretty evident that when Swinburne was in town Howell was at least occasionally one of those who played the part of the flagellant schoolmaster to him, and thus gratified a penchant acquired by the poet during his troublous Eton days."

It is also known that Swinburne some of the material for another Hotten publication, Cooper's *History of the Rod* (although Ashbee identifies the author as James G. Bertram) and contributed regularly to *The Pearl*. In the publisher's advertisements at the rear of the former there was an announcement for the book mentioned in the Howell letter:

The Romance of the Rod: An Anecdotal History of The Birch in Ancient & Modern Times. With some quaint illustrations. Crown 8vo, handsomely printed. (In preparation.)

I have been unable to find any evidence that this book was ever published as Hotten died soon after this announcement appeared.

Given the evidence above, it would be reasonable to speculate that if Hotten had a part to play in his own other flagellation works, then why not the current volume as well? However, Stock refers to a book he is compiling in his letter to William Cooper (quoted above), which could be construed as *The Romance of The Rod*. The most likely conclusion we can come to, therefore, rather than believe the theory that Swinburne and Stock were collaborators, is that Stock supplied material for Hotten, who then commissioned Swinburne to add some of his own accomplished flagellant writing.

A later book was published claiming to be the sequel to *The Romance of Chastisement*, entitled *The Quintessence of Birch Discipline*, though it is unlikely that it came from the same pen—the publisher, hoping, no doubt, to cash in on the current volume's reputation, fabricated this claim to boost his sales.

Whoever the real author is, *The Romance of Chastisement* remains a long neglected classic of English erotic literature, and is deserving of this reprint over 120 years since it first appeared.

MICHAEL R. GOSS
London 1993.

iv

THE

ROMANCE OF CHASTISEMENT;

OR,

Revelations of the School and Bedroom.

BY AN EXPERT.

"EXPERTO CREDE."

" Who, brandishing the rod, doth straight begin
To loose her pants — she trembles with affright —
Adown they drop, appears the dainty skin.
Fair as the furry coat of whitest ermelin."
The Schoolmistress, by Shenstone.

BOSTON:
TREMONT PUBLISHING COMPANY.
1876.

PEN PICTURES;

OR,

HINTS FOR THE FUTURE ILLUSTRATOR OF THE WORK.

FRONTISPIECE.
Le Mauvis Quart d'Heure.

How bad a quarter hour may be we guess
In witnessing this scene of sore distress.
Whirling the rods an angry dame appears,
Aërial shrieks are ringing in our ears;
The butt she aims at is conceal'd by those
Who crowd the foreground cowering in their clothes.
Some clutch their petticoats with nervous twitch
And draw them closer round the threat'n'd breach;
Others, well knowing all resistance vain,
Slowly prepare them for the coming pain.
The twigs fly fast, the terror-teeming text
Issues, unheard by us —
                         " Bring up the next!"

A stout assistant, careless of her cry,
Pops on a pretty Pinfrock standing by;
Her back is to us, ere she can break ground
A pair of purple arms embrace it round,
A fight ensues, the parties pull and bend,
The pink and purple separate and blend;

Accustom'd fingers dart beneath the frock,
The lookers-on anticipate the shock.
Flash goes the white, the nether garments slip,
The pulpy *palimpest* invites the whip —
(A fine word that, it means — she knows how sore
The birch, from having savor'd it before.)
The shift's secured, from forth of it have cropp'd
Flat flesh, tight stockings, and panjammies dropp'd.

In vain the half-choked child for mercy squeals,
And tries to kick her implicated heels;
Vainly her shoulders drag from that embrace,
The lifted bib in vain conceals her face;
Than eye more eloquent the wriggling rear
Collapsed and dimpled, tells of mortal fear.
For that bare back we feel compassion stir,
Nor would we willingly change lots with her.

So far the painter. The spectator's eye,
Roused by his art, th' invisible may spy.
"Look sharp!" —
            By ministering imps propell'd
Before the Fiend, and summarily fell'd,
The plumpest part secured in swerveless fix,
Poor Pinfrock soon shall swallow up her licks.

PROLOGUE FOR PRUDES.

CHASTE ones, of either sex,

Perpend Punch's

"ADVICE TO THOSE ABOUT TO MARRY" ——

and, by the way, the compound monosyllable that followed, elicited, they say, from the humpbacked gentleman a five pound note. Well, substitute

"ADVICE TO THOSE ABOUT TO READ,"

and take the hint. If not, don't blame us.

In the following pages will be found no vulgar words, no blasphemies, no sneers at sacred things. We have but depicted with too graphic pen the accidents of a practice in itself commendable; nay, enjoined. What need to quote King Solomon and Dr. Johnson, sages both?

"Quæ narrare nefas lex tamen esse sinit."

With every desire to treat our subject chastely, we fear it may lead us at times to the confines of fie-fie-ishness. What are we then to do? —

Instead of telling truths in diction terse,
Evade in ambiguity and verse.

Not poetry, mind you, which is quite another affair, but easy colloquial rhymes that won't trouble the reader any more than the spinner. With this view we shall jog along for the most part in five-foot couplets, sometimes alternating the rhymes or altering the measure for variety's sake, but eschewing always the sesquipedalian, that arrantest of shuffles, giving the impression of great go with little effort. Suppose, for instance, we wish to kick up a dust and vanish with clapp'd trap — We take for theme the death of Marcus Curtius——

*　　*　　*　　*　　* 　　(this line is short a third.)
"Waste not your foreign gauds," he cried, as he his courser spurr'd ;
"Rome's richest treasure must be sought not elsewhere than at home,
"'T is he who dares to give *Himself!* an offering for Rome ! "

Plunges slap bang into the closing chasm,
Whereout his soul pops up, tho' Terra has 'em.
In equal spirit of self-off'ring we
Would emulate the deed of Mister C.
A controversy raging at this day
Whether the Birch or Begging's the best way.
(Which following in lady's magazine,
'T were vain to say no bottom can be seen.)
We, nobly daring, jump into the dirt,
Trusting that you 'll remember

THE EXPERT.

THE ROMANCE OF CHASTISEMENT.

INTRODUCTION.

DISCOVERY OF THE MAGIC WAND — CACOETHES FLAGELLANDI — PARLIAMENTARY REPORT OF THE SCHOOL FOR SOLDIERS' DAUGHTERS AT CHELSEA — MISS RAMSBOTTOM THINKS SHE IS TOO OLD — NOUS VERRONS — FAT MACK PAYS FOR PEEPING.

READER,

"Did you ever put a live cat upon its back ? "

"Can't say I did."

"Or try to empty the Atlantic with a teaspoon ? "

"Certainly not."

Just as difficult would it be for any of the profane, who may or may not read these tales, to find the key of knowledge and power which was fortuitously discovered by the narrator.

All who please may accompany us to the margin of the mystery, so near in fact, that each shall cry with the sage of old, or the modern shirt-maker — EUREKA! Yet shall the one supple link that connects *power* with knowledge be wanting. He or she who readeth to the end shall know that there is magic in a birchen wand, and yet not be able to wield it like the Enchanter.

In a broad sense knowledge *is* power; whether it be always a desirable acquisition is another question. At all events, we do not intend in the present instance to betray the mot énigme.

That a prejudice exists in favor of, as well as against, the infliction of birch is undeniable. This feeling is embodied in the following often, but not often correctly, quoted dialogue between

a master manufacturer and his foreman, the true version of which
is as follows : —

Master. "Is it true, Sampson, what I hear, that your wife
licks you ?"

Man. "Ees."

Master. "You ought to be ashamed of yourself. A fellow
with the size of an elephant and the force of a steam-engine, to
let himself be whipt on the tail like a schoolboy — as I 'm told
you do — by a creature he might crack in one fist! Where is
your manhood ? Why do you suffer it ?"

Man. "Whoy ? Well, you see, it pleases her, and it doant
hurt."

The honest Yorkshireman, with all his complaisance for his
little wife, had evidently a practical sense of the delights of
birching, though his dull intellect could not fathom the phenomenon, or explain the discrepancies of a practice, at one time in-
spiring terror and disgust, at another, causing joy all the more
captivating for its vagueness ; uncertain in fact and

> Variable as the maid
> By the light-quivering birches flay'd —

What — whip females at the present day! Impossible! *Et pour
cause?* It *is* done, and done often nearer than you think for.

Assert that foul crimes are perpetuated in the nineteenth
century — no one will contradict you. Say — you have reason
to believe that Mr. A. or Mr. B. — a person intimately known
to your auditor — has been guilty of such, what will be your
reception, unless your allegation be confirmed by the "Horrid
Murder" of the penny-a-liner.

Recognizing this truth, we will address ourselves first to those
prosaic souls who reject all delineations of life by the novelist,
and pin their faith solely to the dicta of the newspapers. We
will show by irrefragable evidence that, in this our day, the rod,
unaccompanied by magnetism, has charms sufficient to induce a
lady of independent means to volunteer to perform the "painful
duty" of the schoolmistress, braving public opinion and risking

her standing in society, for the mere enjoyment of chastising. Now for our matter-of-fact friends.

LADIES AND GENTLEMEN. — We assure you that the article we are about to submit to your notice went the round of the newspapers. It is extracted from a well-known periodical called "Notes and Queries," and the facts therein set forth are supported by parliamentary documents. We give it, heading and all, exactly as it appeared in our evening journal.

"WHIPPING GROWN GIRLS."

"Your correspondent (W. Y S.) may be convinced that the old-fashioned mode of correction for naughty girls by the birch-rod has still its zealous advocates in England, if he will refer to a case brought forward in the House of Commons, June 1, 1863. It related to the discipline of the female school at Chelsea for the daughters of soldiers killed in the Crimean war, which school was founded out of a portion of the Royal Patriotic Fund.

"It appeared that the authorities of the school, the secretary, chaplain, and lady-superintendent, who was the daughter of a naval officer, and a woman of high respectability, approved of this mode of punishment. The girls were whipped by the lady-superintendent, who always inflicted the chastisement with her own hand. Nor did the elder ones escape their liability to this correction. On the contrary, she contended that a girl of fifteen or sixteen both required stricter discipline to keep her in order when she was ill-disposed, and also that the rod had greater terror for her than for a younger child.

"There was a committee of lady visitors, some of whom disapproved of the practice. A keen controversy was carried on. The secretary and lady-superintendent contended that in a school of three hundred girls, many of them sprung from the lower ranks, corporeal correction was absolutely necessary. The ladies who dissented, resigned their duties as visitors, and the whole matter creating some stir, was at last the subject of inquiry and discussion in the House of Commons.

"It ended in a sort of compromise: the birch was discontinued, but the palms of the girls' hands were surrendered to the mercy of the schoolmistresses, who were authorized to inflict strokes with a cane upon them for any offence they might be guilty of."

Courteous reader, what do *you* think of that for a newspaper paragraph? And even that did not tell all. Within the house the case was quoted of a sergeant's daughter, eighteen years of age, who was "flogged like a schoolboy, others looking on." For once the blue-book must have had a piquant page. Permit us the utterance of a few thoughts such as might naturally present themselves to a lively fancy on perusal.

The lady-superintendent was too exclusive. Had she allowed the visitors a fair share in the administration, she would not have been deprived of her wand of office. Monopolizing as she did, she might have guessed it was too good to last.

How pleasant, any fine morning after breakfast, to drive over to the *preserve*, call for the reports of three hundred girls, offering after two days' absence nine hundred chances, and haply including some arch-rebel on whom she has long had an eye; to sentence her and various others to condign punishment; then, preceded by the condemned, and adequate assistants, adjourn to the whipping-room, lock the door against all cavillers, and luxurate in licks, without the bore of having to keep school for it!

A few bribes judiciously administered, would make all safe. Nay, such is the fascination of the birchen sport, the ministrants would soon itch for whipping-time, delight to see a big one get it well, and strip and hold without the least compunction.

The lady's reason for preferring to operate on adults was naïve and suggestive — "the rod has more terror for them than for children." No doubt it had, *mais puis*, Madame? If to cling to the last shift and shout to be let go prove the rod to be terrible to the delinquent, does it not render it all the more racy to the intending whipper, who waits assured the issue of the conflict?

That the soldiers' daughters did not let their tails be seen without a fight is plain, and just as plain that the fight was ineffectual. All were liable to the same correction, and all who deserved it got it indifferently at the hands of the lady-superintendent. Now, before she could have paid them that delicate attention, the "grown girls who most required the rod and most dreaded discipline" must have been either bound to a post, hoisted on a back, or held for her at a convenient angle. There is no romancing here; girls of sixteen to eighteen cannot be birched like babies on the knee, and birched they were somehow, till their cries reached to the House of Commons.

We will assume that they were held on a desk or ottoman, in the manner usual in most boarding schools. And now let us rush, as Horace bids, into the midst of things.

WHIPPING GROWN GIRLS.

(OUR VERSION.)

(The room is lofty, lighted from above. Ten trembling girls are ranged upon a form; a grown-up one stands sulkily aloof. Judgment is being done before their eyes.)

Four stout young women, teachers in the school, crowd round a box-ottoman and press down something in a heap of clothes. A naked end protrudes, to which the lady's arm in vigorous swing applies the birch. Splinters fly round; the walls reverberate with cuts and cries.

(First victim — gathering herself up.)
      "Bellow! — Hullo! — Wullo! — Wc-o-h!
      Sniff — snuffle — sob — sob — sob!"

Lady Sup. "Let that be a lesson to you, Stubbs, how you break plate-glass windows again; your mother must pay half the cost. There, stop that noise. Who's next?"
(First Assistant — reads from a long slip.)

"Ruth Ramsbottom,* sixth class; late in school and insolent to Miss Briggs."

Lady Sup. — *(aside.)* "Which is Ramsbottom?"

First A. "Tall, with black eyes, red Garibaldi and sprigged skirt."

Lady. "*That!* I thought she was the new teacher."

First A. "Only a pupil, ma'am, been away last half."

Lady. "And her name, you say, is in the bill?"

First A. "There it is, No. 2. She did what she liked before you came, so the mistress billed her at once."

Lady. "How did you get her here?"

First A. "On the sly; she knew nothing of the birchings. Give it her well now, we may not have another chance."

Lady. "Hum!—I hardly know—she's as big as you are—her friends might talk."

First A. "Not they, she has no friends; the whole school would like to see her flogged."

Lady. "What did she do?"

---

* NOTE ON MISS RAMSBOTTOM'S NAME.

Although' folks utter them without a stopper,
Their proper names are often most improper;
If spelt correctly, they would make you sick,
Nous passons le chevalier "Chilperic,"
Car ça n'est rien en français, mais "Le Sueur,"
Faugh! fancy kissing her, the thought's impure.
Then—drawn from beercasks or anatomy—
The last 't would seem what countless "cocks" we see
There's Alcock, Smallcock, Hitchcock, Pitchcock, Pocock,
Locock, of course, and even down to Nocock,
And, glorying in their beastly names, odd rot'em!
What topping families protrude the "bottom,"
As for example, Higgin, Winter, Rams,
It may be there are even Trues and Shams.
In short, so much doth use perception blunt,
The wonder is they have n't — *no, I wun't.*

First A. "Said — 'you lie, you b——' to Miss Briggs, quite loud before us all."

Lady. "Aye, aye! shall you be able to hold her though?"

First A. "Well — you see there's four of us."

Second Assistant (who has been bribed.) "Miss Briggs will hold, ma'am, if let; she took sewing class on purpose. Shall I?" *(crosses to door.)*

Lady, (sotto voce.) (That Briggs would be all the better of being whipt herself, a stuck-up thing!) *(Aloud.)* "This is a serious charge. Before I punish a great girl like that, I must have proof that she deserves the rod. Where is Miss Briggs?"

Second A. "Miss Briggs, step in, please. You're wanted." *(Whispering heard without.)*

"That's *her.* No t'aint, that's Susan Stubbs that broke the glass; her shift's pinned up. *My!* look at her behind. Let me see. Look through. Get out of that, you prize pig!"

A fat one tumbles in on all fours, straightens herself on her knees, and stares around half scared, half giggling: a she Sancho with cocked nose and comic eye; at sight of her even the pale convicts brighten up.

Lady. "Hallo! What *is* the meaning of this? Back to your work, all of you. Bolt the door again. Who's that?"

First A. (laughing.) "It's Fat Mack, that is, Mary Mackenzie, ma'am. She *would* come in."

Lady. "So, Miss Mackenzie, you are curious to know what whipping is like?"

Mack (claps her pudgy hands to her behind.) "Na, deed, my leddy, 'twor na me; th' ithers pushed me through the doer."

Lady. "Where you had no business to be. Sit down amongst the rest and wait your turn. Now, which is No. 2, with the odd name?"

The assistants with mocking curtseys indicate Miss R., who snorts and stamps. The lady-superintendent adjusts her eyeglass, and perks her chin, as if about to inspect some entomological variety.

Lady. "Oh, indeed! that fine young lady from the Fashions

Book. Crinoline and Balmorals I declare! But is not the ball
dress somewhat out of place? And that chain, I fear, is but
mosaic. Pity to disarrange so elegant a costume. Perhaps after
all, we may not require the birch. Miss Briggs, pardon me, you
can't be twenty yet, and are too young, I think, for so responsible an office. However, as the Committee thought proper to
appoint you, and you were visitor this morning when — the
Sprigged Muslin there — was billed, be good enough to men-
tion what occurred, confining yourself strictly to the facts at
issue."

Miss Briggs (*looking old with all her might.*) "That girl, Ruth
Ramsbottom, was eight minutes after time."

Ruth. "I was n't."

Miss B. "By the school clock, and called me dog and liar
when I marked her late."

Ruth. "I did n't! You 're telling lies to get me whipped,
you double* b——. How would you like your own tail turned
up before them brats?"

Miss B. "You hear her, ma'am."

Lady. "I do, and so shall you, and hold her if you like."

Ruth. "Who are you? You an't no schoolmistress, and no
lady neither. *Lady* indeed! to lash a poor girl on her *hub-ub-
ub!* (*the Ram bleats.*)

Lady. "I 'll lash *you*, my lady, tight enough. If you *were* a
poor girl, dressed according to your rank in life — but faugh!
you tawdry thing. You, Jackson, hand down the birches from
the top shelf; there are two there with cane handles, bring them
both." Whir-r-r! Whir-r-r! "Ruth Ramsbottom, come here!"

Ruth. "I shan't, it 's a shame, I 'm too old."

Lady. "Too old, are you? We 'll see that presently. Seize
and strip her!"

Casting an appealing look thither, Ruth rushes into the ranks
of the condemned, who all fall from around her or become her

---

* Miss R.'s language was more forcible than polite; the expres-
sions she used were tantamount to sanguineous "she-dog."

active enemies: conspicuous amongst these latter are the whipt one and Fat Mack.   They slip off their garters, jump upon a form, and adroitly catching up the struggler's wrists, secure them together by a double knot.   The trained tormentors then dash in, and in half a crack reduce her to the semblance of an Albanian chief.

> In crimson tunic dight and snowy kilt,
> Lacking but yatagan and poniard hilt.

The strongest, twisting round their hands the aforesaid kilt, employ it as a lever to support the back-thrown bust, and pull her prancing on.

> Vain all her writhings and contortions odd,
> The licking lady with sardonic grin
> Withholds, but only for a space, the rod,
> Watching the happy moment to whip in
> As whip she will, or soon or late, of course,
> Seeing the deadly purpose in her eye,
> Her victim turns the reluctant thigh,
> When down it comes with desolating force,
> And worn to fragments, is again renewed,
> Tho' half a glance the punisher had told
> Before the kicking devil was subdued,
> That Ruth for such correction was too old.

We will now assume that the original twelve culprits have received their dues, meeting their fate, some with the stoicism of foxes, others more or less loudly lamenting.   All have been served save one.   Fat Mack sits on the bench of the condemned — "her leesome lane."   The others have all gathered round the block, anticipating a treat.

The lady principal flings from her the stump of the last rod.

Miss Briggs, to propitiate her, offers one of gigantic proportions, which she has just tied from the least frayed fragments around.

Lady. "Hem! Thank you, Miss Briggs.   You seem to know

the right sort. Got it yourself, belike, not long since. Now
then, don't keep me here all day. Is that girl Mackenzie
ready ? "

Is she? Aye more than ready. The assistants, assuming a
carte blanche, have carried the joke of stripping one of her
peculiar build to the utmost allowable limits. Imagine the
"Bounding Ball of the Pyrénées" in veritable buff, with nothing between the white stockings and the throat save another
narrow strip of white more resembling a cravat than a waistcoat.
To this process of disrobing Fat Mack offers no impediment,
the weather is warm, and clothes to her are only an incumbrance.
When the last pin is fixed, with an indescribable blending of
fright, frolic, and mock modesty, she suffers herself to be dragged
to the fatal spot, where a new spirit seems to enter her.

Mack. "Hooly! Misses baith, slack yer haud o' me. I trow
I'se sort her better nor ye wud yersels."

They let her go, ready to pounce on her again, if need be.

Most of our readers only know the East from description.
Did it ever occur to them to fancy the ridiculous appearance
the performer of a prostration salaam must present to those situ-
ated directly in his or her rear? Even such a posture did Miss
Mackenzie choose to assume in the centre of the ottoman, turning *from* the person saluted the apex of her figure, which, like
a half-inverted pyramid, was completely obscured by the exalted
base. Why did she act thus madly? Why? Impossible to
account for the caprices of a "havrel." That she offered the
accommodation in good faith was plain; she cast no lingering
look behind, but buried her features in the cushion.

The assistants burst into a loud guffaw, the whipt ones stare
aghast. The lady principal starts and flushes to the brow —

> Then, clutching tighter the indignant rods,
> As tip-toe poised, she flings them to the gods.
> Needless to say that the first whack brought down
> The towering mountain level with the plain,
> Tho' the broad bulge between the base and crown
> Caught full the showers of descending pain.

Help us to what a Scot would call a *"semele."*
A cat with Daniel Lambert on her tail?
When told she's ugly or bow-legged Emily?
A butcher'd pig? —
     No, all of these would fail
To reach the echo of the eldritch yell
That followed the first cut, and all that fell.

Yet, when released from the lengthened whipping, Mack, with a "Whoosh!" of relief, faces rubbing round, and addresses her tormentor, when the following dialogue ensues between them.

Mack. "Wow, leddy, but yer han' is sair, and yon is hetter than the taws!"

Lady. "Let it be a lesson to you then not to peep through keyholes without leave again.   Turn t'other way, and get yourself unpinned."

Mack. "Yes, m'm, no m'm.   Please, m'm, *may* I peep through next whuppin day?"

Lady. "Certainly not.   If your conduct be such as to merit chastisement, you can enter with the rest, and see and be seen without hindrance.   Did you hear what I—"

Mack. "Ye munna lick me *here*, it's ower sair."

Lady. "Sore!   My object is to make the whipping sore; yours should be, by discreeter conduct to avoid a repetition.

  "Go, Miss, remember you are bare,
   Or d'ye want some more already?"
       (Shakes the rods at her.)

Mack (retreating)
  "A weel, ise gie ye t'ither fair,
   And do yer warst, ahint me, leddy."

It was cruel of parliament to interfere with the good lady's labour of love and spoil the sport of her assistants; the more so as there was no true charity in the decision arrived at.   The Chelsea schoolgirls, we will be bound to say, found the unrestricted canes of all the schoolmistresses a worse infliction than occasional interviews, however exciting, with the "Admiral's Daughter."

We admit that the foregoing is a fancy sketch *quoad* the Chelsea school-room. Be it remembered, however, that we could not have described these things *never seen*. Even the most prosaic must allow that our mock details are justified by the premises. Having shown that such things are, and proved our point, we would bespeak a full measure of credit for the following Tales, which are based on an experience so wide and comprehensive as to warrant the title we have assumed of

THE EXPERT.

PEN PICTURES.

No. II.

THE AWFUL PAUSE.

KIND Mrs. Van., her back by pillows stayed
　　The silver curls adorning her fair face,
Awaits in bed the advent of the maid
　　Prompt ministrant of dolour and disgrace.
Time flies — to *her* of painful scenes afraid
　　It presses with accelerated pace ;
Her open watch upon the table near
Tick-tics — too soon the switches will appear.

The culprit, cock'd up on the window-stool
　　Facing her grandmother, with careless sway
Lollops her legs and feigns to be quite cool,
　　Distending them as widely as she may.
The shameless action shows — * the want of rule
　　And need of the "new leaf." Far flung away
Her slighted hymn-book in the corner lies,
Thro' ebon locks she glares with panther eyes.

To say a simple verse, to come at call,
　　Are simple things to do, yet well I wiss
Her silly pride will bring about a fall
　　Such as doth go before the birch's kiss ;

---

* Hint to the Artist. —
　　　　The lady 's opposite, remember. *We*
　　　　But catch the flopping of the frock-clad knee..

When the avenger, truculent and tall,
  Swings high her arm for what to her is bliss,
Wo worth the day! if, pants and shimmy gone,
That heavy hand be licensed to lay on.

Confess, Miss Kathleen, that your pulse beats odd,
  Your garments cling to you with pressure rare,
While giant Stiles is fetching the birch rod
  Designed to act upon — you best know where.
Since pardon you won't sue for, at a nod
  Strong hands will bend you blubbering and bare;
The rest *may* follow — should by all the laws —
Won't something tingle in that *"Awful Pause?"*

THE CLOSE SHAVE.

A Tale in One Chapter.

To cut a long story short is the best policy, especially where
expectations are doomed to be disappointed, as your's, reader,
we warn you will be, if you go on with the present "ower true
tale."

Ann Stiles, notwithstanding her commonplace designation,
was a tall and stylish-looking damsel, who, on attaining her
eighteenth birthday, had been promoted from the village school
to the dignity of own maid to Mrs. Vansittart.

And who was she? Mrs. Vansittart, called for shortness Mrs.
Van., was the loveliest old lady your eyes ever looked on. Her
dresses, of rich materials, were cut in the mode prevalent some
sixty years ago, when our grandmothers, like ourselves, were
naughty. Time with its whirligig brings fashions round; hoop,
bustle, or crinoline, all will come *round* at last. We shall not
enter into details of Mrs. Van.'s belongings, taking warning from
the bévue of a popular writer, whose last novel we glanced at
only this morning. He tells us in his first page that "Miss
Biddy Forbisher" wore a jacket with broad buttons, a hat, a
collar and necktie; he then added that boots and beaver gloves
completed "a costume which was admirably adapted" — Thank
you, we know what *it was* adapted for. Mrs. Van.'s hair, luxu-
riant and white as snow, was tastefully arranged under a lace
cap. above and around a plump comely face that bloomed only
with the natural rose, and had a patch here and there to set off

its fairness. Her eyes were still bright, her teeth pearly; and like Annie Laurie she had "a low sweet voice," with which she would warble ditties quaint and tender as the warbler.

> "There *was* a time, there *was* a time
> When *I* was young and gay!"

Though she sang this with a smile, it brought tears to the listener's eyes, who looking at the evening beauties of her face, could see how exquisitely fair had been the morning. She was cheerful, hospitable, charitable, and pious without pretension. She lived in an old manor-house in Old England; all the old squires were her lovers still, and all her young neighbors called her grandmama.

The only two who might rightly address her by that title were Hedworth and Kathleen Kennedy. Mrs. Vansittart's daughter and sole child married Don Enrico Kennedy, a Spanish Irishman, who, settling in Madrid after his wife's decease, confided his children, at her own earnest request, to the care of their English grandmother.

Hedworth was near seventeen, his form was fast filling up, and the silky fringe to his cheeks betokened incipient manhood. He had little of the shyness incidental to that age, his merry blue eye being full of fun and devilry. To a young lady he might perhaps hesitate to tell his tale of love, but with Ann Stiles he had no such scruple. With her he had long established kissing relations, and not satisfied with that, was importunate for further favours. Read on, and you will find how a pin's point may decide whether he shall succeed in obtaining them.

Kathleen was an unbroken colt, with flowing black mane and flashing eyes, who looked as though she had never had on curb or saddle. To drop the language of the stable, she was a child you would stop to stare at in the street, thinking her of gipsy blood and the makings of a Beauty. She was big for her age, being by three and a half years Hedworth's junior. Grandmama doted upon both: of the two, Kathleen, from her greater resemblance to her handsome father, was probably the favourite. The old lady had indulged her into a rank rebel and household plague, and being conscientious as kind, had serious thoughts of turning over a new leaf — if possible.

> "Kathleen, Mavourneen,
> Awake from your slumbers!"

and turn out like a bagged fox for our diversion.

In all our experiences there are certain days which we commence, as it were, left leg foremost, and everything goes contrary. In such a mood Miss Kennedy arose one bitter east-windy morning, her ill-humour aggravated by Stiles, who, for reasons of her own, suggested every mortifying topic she could think of while assisting at the young lady's toilet. She contrasted, for instance, the little notice taken of her (Kathleen) with the homage universally accorded to her grandmother.

"Ah! miss, you would n't be so proud of yourself, if you seen Square Harbottle's face yesterday when you refused to come at her bidding. After your back was turned he shook his whip at you — did the squire?"

"He did 't, you 're a fibber; he kissed me going out, as he always does."

"Hoity, toity! you had best be civil in the next room; your gran'ma won't stand much more of your cheek, I promise you. Sit down to your hymn, and mind you say it better than you did yesterday — or "

And Stiles went out with a mocking laugh, clapping her palms together to intimate correction in a certain quarter.

Now of all her tasks this hymn-saying was the one most repugnant to the fast-growing girl; not from any special dislike to sacred things, but because, with the sensitiveness of thirteen to fourteen years, she deemed the performance derogatory to her dignity of young lady. Mrs. Van. seldom rose till mid-day, and before going down to make the tea Kathleen had to stand by her bedside and repeat some dozen lines of pious platitudes. It riled her sore; her grandmother, unwitting the cause of her dislike, insisted on the customary task, and by this road both

were rapidly approaching to the inevitable rod question.   The
advice in to-day's portion : —

> "But children, you should never let
> Such angry passions rise,
> Your little hands," &c. ——

had anything but a sooth-
ing effect; in fact it brought matters to a crisis.

"Bah! what beastly bosh it is! I won't put up with it any
longer."

With this resolve she entered with a scowl, declined the proffered kiss, and so conducted herself as to ruffle even the sweet
temper of Mrs. Van., and to force that lady to think of the
"new leaf" with ominous distinctness.

"How dare you, child, behave to me with such disrespect?
Stand up, take your hands out of your pockets, and repeat your
hymn."

"I won't. I'm too big to be made say verses like a baby."

"You won't! Is this proper language to me? Now listen,
Kathleen, for I'm in earnest. I warned you yesterday that, if
this occurred again, I would make Stiles whip you. She is willing to do so, and has the rod prepared : beg my pardon and say
your hymn, else I shall ring the bell and bid her fetch it.

"I don't care, I won't say such silly stuff, and you need not
try to make me, for I *won't* do it."

"Will you beg my pardon ? "

"*No!* — whip indeed! I'll slap Stiles well if she dares to
lay a finger on me."

"Tush child, that is the rankest nonsense, Stiles will have
my orders for what she does, and you'll find she won't be trifled
with. O Kathleen, you have never been punished yet, you
don't know what it is to be whipped with a birch rod. Think
of the disgrace, the pain — and what it will cost me to see you
beaten, and not be able to interfere consistently with my duty
as a Christian parent! Must I ring? Stay, it wants five minutes to nine; I will give you till then to think better of it."

So saying, she laid her massive gold watch upon the table where it could be seen by both. The rebel flung her Watts into a corner, folded her arms, and seated herself, legs up, on the window stool. The short frock scarce covered her lollopping legs, and she faced the old lady, who, recalling the different manners of her day, shook her head and sighed remorsefully.

A pause issued big with the fate of Kathleen Kennedy. Had the maid been tender-hearted as the mistress, the upshot would have been of little moment, but such was far from being the case. Only lately emancipated herself from birchen rule, Miss Stiles gloried in the acquisition of the right end of the rod, and the privilege to whip a lady. A gentleman would have pleased her better still, but Hedworth was out of the question. While binding the branches of the stinging birch and visiting the rod when made, she had pampered her fancy with visions of reddening flesh, kicking limbs, and shouts of pain under the cuts inflicted by herself in requital for sundry slaps bestowed on her by Kathleen, who by the way, might as well have contended with an elephant. Stiles stood five feet ten in her stocking soles; "Granny's Grenadier" Hedworth called her; her will was strong, her arm muscular and brawny. Hitherto tyrant Kathleen had fought under the ægis of her grandmother; if Stiles be now licensed to lay on, it will indeed be *Væ victis!*

The last seconds of the fifth minute are fleeting —

> "Oh! why art thou silent,
> Thou voice of my heart?"

When the long hand had clearly passed the ninth figure, the bell was rung.

"O Ann, how quick you are! I sent for you — that is — Miss Kathleen, I am sorry to say, has been naughty, and won't say her hymn, or even beg my pardon. Ahem! Have you made the rod as I desired you?"

"Yes, ma'am, made it the same day; it's in my box, shall I fetch it?"

"Do so; if she does not repent meantime, I must get you to whip her."

Away flew Ann on the wings of desire, re-entered demurely, and looked around to see if all were safe.

Mrs. Van. had apparently been weeping. At sight of the rod she started and murmured a faint remonstrance against its size. Kathleen, enthroned in sullen state, did not deign to turn her head. Her bust was shrouded by the sable locks, from forth which her eyes, fierce as a panther's, glared upon her grandmother: the latter returned a meek imploring glance — in vain.

With a whispered caution to Ann not to strain the child's back, and a loud one to wait for the signal, Mrs. Van. turned her face to the wall, held back a trembling hand over the bedside for about twenty seconds — groaned — and let fall her handkerchief.

In less than the time named the gigantic abigail had knocked every breath of wind out of the fractious child and torn her in pieces —

> Ann lifts her left leg on a lounging chair,
>   And over it she turns, as you may guess,
> The part she wants, exalted in the air,
>   Split, equipoised, and destitute of dress,
> The end that should be upper, so no more,
> Is pendent now, black curls strew the floor,
> And tho' "our love is but a lassie yet,"
> We faintly trace a stencilling of jet.
>
> Fixing her eyes on this as on a charm,
>   "Sweetly I'll switch," Ann murmurs, "spite her jigs.
> Missis mayhap may stop me in alarm,
>   As squeal the young 'un will, no doubt, like pigs.
> This cut at least shall do the utmost harm
>   To that that's visible between the riggs.
> Here goes!" she swings aloft her brawny arm
>   And ——
>   No, alas! she don't —
>   bring down the twigs.

The fat parson, who, with the first cut of the haunch upon his fork, was arrested by apoplexy ere he could convey the savoury morsel to his mouth, was hardly dealt with by fate. Scarce less pitiable was the plight of Stiles, her arm arrested in the act of striking.

Brief as had been the interval between sentence and execution, it was prolonged by the presence of a headless pin which kept one lobe of the pink flesh still covered with white calico. The search for this pin which ensued, and the pricking it occasioned, enabled Kathleen to reflect on the folly of her conduct in trusting a part so tender to the mercy of her foe, when so little was needed to protect it. Up to the last moment she had counted on her grandmother's relenting. Now, with the birches whistling o'er her tail, she utters a short sharp cry of protest. "Songs without words" may be fanciful appeals, but there is that in the cry of *real fright* which cannot be mistaken.

At the sound the old lady starts upon her seat, and takes in the peril at a glance. Forgetting the burden of her fourscore years, she tumbles from the bed and catches the uplifted arm, while shrieking out a veto.

"Stop, Stiles! Stop, I bid you! Yah! You'd kill the child. There, that will do. O my heart, how it beats! Button up, Kathleen, and let it be a warning to you, for depend on it — Well, what are *you* waiting for? Go at once, you cruel girl, and take away that thing. A savage would blush to use it as you were going to when I stopped you."

Stiles opens her mouth, shuts it, shakes her head and departs, bearing with her the disparaged rod, to be reconsigned to durance, probably for ever.

On her way through the lobby, Hedworth, issuing from his room in frolic mood, springs on Ann and salutes her. Feeling a roughness where all should have been soft and round, he draws forth the armed hand from beneath the apron.

"Hallo! Big 'un, what have you been a doing of with that ere thundering persuader?"

"The mistress sent for me to whip Miss Kathleen."

"Hurrah! so my lady has caught it at last. Did you give it her sweetly ? "

"No, that I did n't."

"Why not ? She wanted it badly enough, I know."

"She did not like it all the same — sang out to stop! and the blessed old lady would n't let me strike her."

"Precious disappointed you don't look neither ! "

"So I am — a toad. Plague take her! she'll be worse now than ever. Her pants down and all, and she bold as brass, only frightened of the rod at the last moment."

"Small blame to her. By jingo, there's an arm ! "

And pulling up the loose sleeve, he bared it to the shoulder. Then seeing tears of disappointment on her flushed cheeks, he kissed them off, and whispered : —

"Look here, Ann, I'll tell you what it is. I owed more for billiards then I let on to Gan, and have not a rap left. Give me that crownpiece I saw in your workbox, and you shall take down my breeches, lay me on your lap, and birch me on the bare till all is blue."

"O Hedworth! are you in earnest? You shall have the crown and welcome, you dear boy. Often as I was punished and helped to hold other girls, I never had the rod in my own hands till this morning — and now I want *so* to whip in earnest, as tight I mean as we used to get it from Dame Dobbs. *Will* you let me ? "

"Will I ? *Won't I ?* Turn in and try, that's all."

And that is all.

Save that Miss Stiles lost more than her crownpiece, and found to her cost that tail-tickling with a lusty youth is a dangerous game to play at —

> "For gowd rings ye may buy, maidens,
> And kirtles ye may spin,
> But gin ye lose yer — What-ye-ca'ems,
> Ye'll ne'er get *thot* again."

In the Scotch song the lost article is called by its proper name: we, however, are resolved to be "severely proper."

PEN PICTURES.

No. III.

LITTLE THINGS.

"Ah! little things bring back to me,"
 Sings Mabel, stretch'd to suit,
As, rocking Jacky on her knee,
 She plays the magic flute.
Dora, her spirits all afloat,
 Looks on but to admire,
While sneaking Steinkopf takes the note
 Will set her tail a-fire.

The limner, cunning in his trade,
 Must here some art employ
To sketch the nimble-finger'd maid
 And blushing bare-breech'd boy.
Her scarlet-petticoat may glow,
 His lily limbs be seen;
Mais ce qu'il n'est pas comme il faut
 A peindre, s'imagine.

Patience; we promise you shall see,
 Or *partly* hear some day
The price that for their shameless spree
 These naughty ones must pay.

Dora, the school-girl, shall kneel
  (Next Plate) in deep distress;
But Mabel, mettled maid, will feel
  More than we dare express.

At present, pretermitting sighs,
  The frolic Muse but sings
Of laughing lassies, lullabies,
  And other "Little Things,"
That deftly dandled into baby powers,
Bring back to Mabel "thoughts of bygone hours."

REVELATIONS OF SHREWSBURY HOUSE,

IN A
LETTER FROM DORA DOVETON TO HER COUSIN,
MRS. SLINGSBURY, IN AUSTRALIA.

A Tale in Two Parts.

PART FIRST.

CHAPTER I.

MRS. MARTINET — ROD-MAGNETISM.

THE task you have assigned me, dear Jacintha, though a laborious, is not an ungrateful one. In your far Australian home you receive a newspaper, new at least to you, in which the year old scandals of the Shrewsbury House are mentioned as a thing of yesterday. Remembering that I was an inmate about that time, (fortunate for me, I had left before the esclandre) you ask me to narrate the events so obscurely hinted at exactly as they occurred, and specially to note the impressions made by them on me; with a flattering reference to my supposed graphic powers.

Repeating that I was not present at the time of the break-up, I will endeavor to comply with your request for both our sakes, while those impressions are fresh upon my mind: a few months hence the novel duties of a wife will probably have weakened them. I wish I were able to do more justice to my theme, for the annals of Shrewsbury House are worth preserving.

To an attentive observer the world seems distressingly full of action.

> Scarce can the weary senses pause,
> So quick th' events to trace their cause.

Yet what proportion does the recorded bear to the waveless sea of histories that have perished for want of a recorder?

Relying on your promise that what I write shall be for you alone, I shall speak with as much freedom as we used together in the days of our greatest intimacy.

Even the meagre sketch in the "Times" must have shown you that the Rod, and its wielder, Martinet, will be prominent features in my story. I proceed therefore to introduce them specially, commencing with the passive instrument.

When the savage corrects his wife with a stick he does so with the sole notion of punishing. It is simply a beating, such as would be inflicted on any of the lower animals. How widely different does the case become, when for the club of the savage is substituted the graceful birch which tortures without injuring; and when, previous to the punishment, the clothes of civilization are removed, not from the back — that would be much — but because it is more accessible, from one of the most secret parts, the accessories too generally involving the exposure of *the* most secret part of the person! Strange that woman should converse so coolly, even with each other, of having whipped, endured, or witnessed a whipping; without reflecting on what the feelings of a man would be, or their own, were a man present during the operation. Between the sexes the subject is rarely alluded to; never, I think, without a conscious glance, or a smile maybe, if the degree of intimacy warrant it.

Such is the indelicate entourage of a whipping, making it sacred even when viewed in the most commonplace light. But, Jacintha, there is another aspect connected with magnetism or electricity, subjects which I do not profess to understand, much less explain to others. You and I are, however, aware that, where there is a predisposition in the subject, a strong will can subdue a weaker, transmitting by passes of the hand a subtle fluid from the one body to the other, and conveying by the same channel its own volition to the mind of the recipient, who is thenceforth its slave. This is undeniable; hundreds besides ourselves have witnessed the apparent miracle.

Now, consider the superior predisposing causes in the case of punishment with the rod ; the will of the whipper intensified to avenge, the mind of the culprit prostrated in most instances by fear and shame, two of the strongest passions; while the channel of communication, instead of being simple passes of the hand, is the Rod, writing its laws in characters of blood. The fancy of the whipper is generally filled at the time with prurient images, and if he or she possess the power of projecting the electric, or other fluid, it will produce on the person whipt the extraordinary effects which I shall particularize further on.

There are, I hope and believe, very few persons who possess this power of rod-magnetism. It was, however, my lot, and that of most of my companions, to encounter such a one in the person of our preceptress, Mrs. Martinet, of Shrewsbury House. Never was will so intensified as hers; she could have looked down a bull in mid career, and this strong will was seconded by a commanding figure and great bodily powers. At some period of her career, probably an early one, she might have been initiated herself by a rod-magnetiser; certainly during the whole term of our acquaintance, to whip girls was her ruling passion. She never betrayed any partiality for the society of men, but used her purse and great powers of fascination to the one end of surrounding herself with the loveliest of her own sex, on whom she exerted her magnetical influence.

You will naturally ask how, in civilized England, such a tyranny could have been endured so long; and you will be surprised when I inform you that we — we, the victims, were her firmest allies. The preliminaries to the first whipping were as shocking and repulsive as, I presume they must be in ordinary cases; but after the infliction of a few stripes, her magic rod when she so willed, would infallibly communicate her own lusts to the sufferer, who would then glory in ministering to them. We, — here perhaps I had better speak for myself alone — I then never lost my terror of the rod, yet doted on the hand that wielded it, as if it were a lover's, and in the very agony of dis-

cipline would seek to gratify my tormentress by the freest display of my naked person.

One little, or rather great, personal peculiarity I may add, to
bring Mrs. Martinet more vividly before you. That part of her
pupil's figures with which she most loved to deal, was, in her
own, so remarkably developed, she had no need to resort to
the then prevalent fashion to give the *idea* of rotundity in that
quarter, and preferred wearing her skirts fitted to her person.
I think I see you smile at *my* noticing this fact.

In finishing the mental portraiture of this extraordinary woman, it is only fair to add that she was strictly impartial, never
punishing without just cause, or provoked misconduct by caprice
or ill-temper. The almost princely liberality of her establishment was the admiration of all beholders. To us, though never
affectionate, she was generous, and would frequently recompense
those she handled the worst by some rich gift without reference
to the cause that produced it.

CHAPTER II.

The Journey — Shropshire — A "Dream of Ludlow Castle."

When my father left us to resume his diplomatic functions
at Vienna, it was resolved that my mother should join him there
after her confinement, and that during the three or four years
they must needs reside abroad, my education should be continued
at an English boarding-school. Our means being ample, no
other school of course could be thought of than the celebrated
Shrewsbury House in the next county. By a fortunate accident,
room for one pupil happened to be vacant at the time, and to
secure this it was necessary that I should set out immediately.

As dear mamma was unable to accompany me, Mrs. Goodwin
was sent, carrying with her a letter of introduction and a con-
siderable sum, £150 I think it was, to pay for my first half-year
in advance. We travelled in the barouche with our own horses

for the first stage, and afterwards posted, the total distance being about forty miles. At Leominster we lunched; shortly after
which ceremony old Goodwin, you remember her somnolent
habits, fell into a doze which was not likely to be disturbed for
some time, and I amused myself with anticipations of my future
home and companions.

I was soon attracted by the beauty of the scenery through
which we were passing. Shropshire, the largest of the midland
counties, is of an oblong form, and split into nearly equal parts
by the river Severn, which is navigable for a great part of its
course. Though the oak woods of Salop have long supplied the
wants of the Bristol ship-builders, they are still prolific and
flourishing. These sylvan scenes witnessed the final encounter
of the Britons with the Romans; a place in this county, called
Caer Caradoc, is still pointed out as the traditionary site of the
last action. Caractacus's speech, when carried prisoner to
Rome, has been preserved by the historian Tacitus, and if the
translation I read be a faithful one, it is a model of manly eloquence, showing that noble hearts have felt the same in all ages.
More than twelve centuries later, the oak of Boscobel, also in
this county, gave shelter to the royal fugitive Charles.

Of all its noteworthy objects the tower of Ludlow Castle, near
which we entered the county, interested me most. That dis-
mantled pile was long the seat of the lord wardens, who held
courts there for the settlement of all matters connected with
the marches; and within its walls Milton's masque of Comus
was first enacted by the children of the Earl of Bridgewater, the
president of the county. More than this, the young King Edward
V. and his brother the Duke of York lived there, in that very
Castle of Ludlow, under the protection of Earl Rivers, till their
removal by order of the Duke of Gloucester, afterwards Richard
III., to the Tower of London.

We are accustomed to consider these unfortunate princes as
mere infants; but chronicles state that the eldest at least was
well grown, and as he "held court" at Ludlow, it is to be pre-
sumed he had become attached to life ere he was forced to quit

it in so painful a manner. What a brief old-world tragedy that
was, and still so full of interest as to occupy thoroughly the mind
of the modern traveller. Emulating Goodwin, that tranquil
specimen of the nineteenth century, I lay back in my corner of
the carriage, where I too had my *réverie, que voilà.*

A DREAM OF LUDLOW CASTLE.

Methought, as I nodded, that centuries roll'd
  Far back thro' the slumbering highway of time,
All was silence and void, save a whisper that told
  Some vague revelation of splendour and crime.

The darkness of midnight that first settled down
  On the gloaming horizon was suddenly clear'd.
Embattled aloft o'er the President's town
  Lys Dinan, the Palace of Princes, appear'd.

The far-flashing light from the casement that shone,
  Attracted my spirit. I entered the hall.
There were beauties fair Dreamland can furnish alone,
  And music that waking ears vainly recall.

Earl Rivers the courtly presented a child
  In form, yet a maiden whose love-smother'd fire
The downy-cheek'd monarch, all joyous and wild,
  Flashed back with the chivalrous glance of his sire.

Oh! brief was that vision of glory. Anon
  The darkness returned with sevenfold power.
The lineage of Edward the Gallant is gone.
  Night whisper'd the deed that was done in the Tower.

The county town had for some time receded on our left, and
we had been gradually tending upward and eastward towards
the Wrekin, a hill which rises singly out of the plain to a height
of twelve hundred feet above the level of the Severn, and commands some of the richest and most varied scenery in England.
Another turn of the road brought us in sight of the Shrews-

bury House as the setting sun was gilding its numerous turrets.

I may as well describe the building now, though it took me days to understand its complex structure. It was of a castellated form, exhibiting at each side of the main entrance a suit of lanceolate windows, each row separated from its lateral neighbour by an ivy-covered buttress : the whole line was flanked by battlemented towers. Great as was its apparent size, that was still deceptive, for the central part was double-bodied, the rearmost building being uninhabitable, or at least uninhabited. An eccentric member of the Talbot family, once the mainstay of the English Roman Catholic interest, had chosen to construct a modern mansion in front of a forsaken nunnery, using its chapel only for devotional purposes. By degrees this too fell into desuetude, and after various changes the modern part was converted into a ladies' boarding-school.

Mrs. Martinet, hearing it was for disposal closed at once with the terms, and by the aid of her taste and purse had beautified and enlarged it, preserving, however, the original character of the building. The offices, which had formed rectangular wings, she replaced by additional dormitories, and had built new stables at a distance, and screened off from the main building where none but females were suffered to reside. Her domains indeed were as strictly guarded as the gardens of the Hesperides we used to read of in Lemprière. Wherever nature had not presented a barrier she had surrounded them with lofty walls. The rear was altogether inaccessible, for, from the terrace behind the old building the ground sank in a sheer bramble-clad descent of many feet to a lake of treacherous depth. Beyond this was an orchard which could be reached only by a locked postern. Through the orchard was a pathway leading to a village which supplied the house with common articles of consumption or dress, the rarer being sent for, when required, to Shrewsbury.

CHAPTER III.

THE ARRIVAL — HELEN MACGREGOR — INTRODUCTION TO MRS.
MARTINET — THE SUPPER TABLE.

As we neared the house two tall girls were playing La Grâce
upon the lawn, surrounded by a circle of their companions,
whose attention was so fixed on the flying hoops they did not
perceive our approach till we were close upon them. The larger
of the two then came up with a cordial smile and greeted me
thus: —

"Shake hands first, whoever you are. You, I presume, are
Miss Doveton, I am Helen Macgregor, and if you are Doveton,
you are to be my chum, for there is no other room with a bed
vacant except Miss De Vere's; but we will talk of that presently."

Observing Mrs. Goodwin for the first time, she apologized
bluntly but kindly, and committed the old lady to the care of
the housekeeper.

"Now, then, Miss Doveton — but are you Doveton? for ye
did na tell me."

"Yes," I replied, "I am Dora Doveton."

"Dora Doveton, what a pretty name, and — but come awa,
my bonny doo, ye'll just hae time to tidy yersel and visit Her
Majesty before tea, where ye'll sit next me. But take a look
now, and mind you know me again, for there's a lot of us, I promise you."

I obeyed, and saw before me a handsome black-eyed girl,
whose age I could not guess she was so rapidly developing into
woman. Broad shouldered she was and large of limb, with
regular features and a general expression of frankness and high
spirit. She showed me the way to our joint bedroom, where
my trunk had already been placed, and bidding me ring if I
required anything, considerately left me to my reflections.

Without Helen's assurance that it was so, I could not have
imagined so sumptuous an appartment destined for my use. It

was richly carpeted, and had mirrors that reflected the whole person. The walls were panelled with oak and supported a few beautiful oil paintings, evidently the work of masters. Though it might have accommodated many sleepers, the room had only two beds, one a solid four-poster, the other a specimen of French upholstery, whose gilded pole and graceful fall of purple silk, contrasting with the snowy linen, made one long for bed-time to enjoy it. Near this was a Spanish mahogany wardrobe, empty and invitingly open, showing by its position that the tent-bed was intended for me. There were chests of drawers besides, and all appliances for comfort and luxury, including a bath-room with marble basin and pipes for hot and cold water. Girandoles with wax candles, silver standishes on the writing tables, all, even to the minutest details, bespoke taste unchecked by any considerations of economy.

You may suppose, dear Jacintha, it was not without a palpitating heart I first found myself in the presence of the mistress of all this splendor; and when I saw her the accessories seemed quite in keeping with her regal port and manner. She was a large woman, scarce past the prime of life, and still handsome; though few, I think, ever ventured to criticise very closely her features. Her dresses were always of the richest materials, and she had a weakness for jewelry and perfume.

On my entrance she started with a smile of pleased surprise, almost of recognition. I half hoped she was about to claim me for an acquaintance, but her cold gray eye soon resumed its normal expression. She made me sit beside her, and addressed to me such polite inquiries as the circumstances warranted; told me that, if she and I wished it, Goodwin might remain the whole of the next day, as business would not be resumed till the following one; and that in the interim I must trust to Miss Macgregor to give me the carte du pays. She then invited me to accompany her to the tea-room. As we approached, and the rustle of her silk dress was heard, a hubbub of noisy laughter and objurgation that prevailed was stilled at once to the tones of polite society.

I must ask you, dear, to take a peep with me through the entrance, that you may have at least a general idea of my dramatis personæ. How many myriad scratches of the pen it takes to convey even the faintest image of what the eye with a single wink finds printed on the retina !

It is eight o'clock of a fine evening in autumn, and many of the windows are still open. You see before you a table extending the whole length of the room, brilliantly lighted with globe lamps, and covered with a sumptuous repast, for our queen is taut soitpeu gourmande, and her subjects are quite willing to follow her example. The table is divided at stated intervals by silver urns, each presided over by a teacher or monitress. As, when all are assembled, the pupils amount to the number of four score, it would be vain for me to attempt particular description : about them all there was a marked patrician air, and any girl who was plain in face was sure to have some compensating charm of person. Having said so much, I shall now sketch only two or three of the presiding nymphs of the urn.

Nearest to us is Madamè Renardeau, a southern Frenchwoman, sallow and swarthy as usual, yet looking handsome in some inexplicable way that only such creatures can accomplish. She has a tendency to embonpoint, which she endeavors to restrain by tight lacing, not to the improvement of her temper. She has also a pair of bright cruel-looking black eyes, and another expression I could not then define, but remarked at times on the faces of many of the company.

Below her, on the opposite side, is Fräulein Steinkopf, the German teacher ; a blonde, who would be pretty, but for a restless prying air : she has the reputation of being a spy, and is avoided by all but her own clique.

Very different is her opposite neighbor, Miss Armstrong, the assistant English teacher, a good-humoured girl of two or three and twenty, who might be selected as the type of a large section of her countrywomen. Undeniably handsome she is, but it is a coarse animal style of beauty ; a splendid fleur de *lit*, but no more. Her name is an appropriâte one — she is strong of arm, and can pull the heaviest girl in the school across a line. This of course I found out afterwards.

I might go on to describe many more, into whose mouths, after the manner of novelists, I know I should put pretty speeches àpropos of nothing. But I only profess, in compliance with my Jacintha's request, and with just as much of setting as is consistent with truth and nature, to depict certain facts which of themselves will be found sufficiently strange and striking.

I must not conclude my peep into the tea-room without remarking that this fair company was waited on by a bevy of parlour-maids, all more or less remarkable for good looks, and dressed after the manner of stage soubrettes. Not one of them but had her chemisette of lawn, her laced apron and cambric pocket handkerchief, the latter article scented by express desire of her mistress.

Being willing through fatigue to escape from the crowded panorama, and having ascertained that I might do so from Helen, who kissed me and promised to respect my slumbers at ten, I slipped off to my pretty purple couch, and was asleep in a few moments.

CHAPTER IV.

BATH AND BED — INKLINGS — PATTY WILKINS' BUDGET.

"Bright chanticleer proclaims the dawn,
And spangles deck the sky."

In all the gamut of sound there is none more suggestive than the shrill clarion of the cock, speaking of the life before life when hinds and milkmaids have the young fresh world to themselves. It is doubly pleasant, too, in the springtide of youth and hope, to be recalled by it from Dreamland in a strange room. The window should be there; in its place a congeries of hoops and a dress that is evidently not mine. The light too comes from another quarter; travelling in search of it, my eye falls upon a bed, open at the foot, and revealing a pillow strewed with jetty curls. The black hair recalls the image of Helen Macgregor — aye, I am Dora Doveton, but this is Shrewsbury House, not home.

The French clock on the mantle-piece strikes five ; now for the luxury of a bath while I may enjoy it alone. I closed the door of communication very gently for fear of disturbing Helen. Even in solitude I felt alarmed, and turned from the marble sarcophagus, lest when I had released the imprisoned flood, I should be unable to arrest its course. But there are cans of cold water, bath pans, gigantic sponges, and towels of every size and hue.

The pressed fungus was sending its welcome river down my back, which was towards the bedroom, when I heard a chirping sound like a kiss, and turning, beheld Helen's laughing face with a "May I come in ?" at the open door. I answered in the affirmative, but stepped quickly out of the pan and covered myself with a sheet.

"Now, Dora," she remonstrated in a half pettish tone, "I did not mean to disturb you ; if you really don't wish me to enter, say so, and I will wait till you have done."

"Oh, no !" I replied, "only I thought perhaps you might think it wrong."

"Think it wrong, you silly puss ! There (bolting the door,) you see we two girls are alone. Maybe you thought that because I am so big I must be a man. Why did you not use the bath ? "

"I was afraid of the stiff cock," I replied.

"Eh ! troth I b'lieve ye, lass ; it 's little ye ken of stiff cokes, as ye ca'em, and they 're kittle cattle to steer for them that doo."

Helen rarely spoke Scotch, and only under protest as it were, to her best friends : As she did so now, it sounded so funny and she made so droll a grimace withal, I could not help a hearty laugh, and though I felt myself still blushing, I did not resist her any more.

She, meanwhile, was quite at home among the brazen cocks, turning them alternately until the reservoir was nearly full. There was ample room for both, and we splashed and revelled together till the increasing chill warned us it was time to restore the circulation by friction with a coarse towel. That done, Helen laid an embargo on our shifts, and proposed that ere resuming them, we should finish the process by warming in her bed.

"There is a good half-hour yet before first bell; besides Martinet said I was to give you the carte du pays. Jump in and hug me tight."

"Plus proche est la peau que la chemise," says a French proverb; here was I that had been dreading a stiff reception, already embracing the naked person of the senior girl in the school. It is so pleasant, too, that cuddle after a bath. At first, though impressionable, all feels cold and hard, like living marble, if such there were; presently the close contact of the vitals, and the commingling breath, send the current racing through the veins, and we are soft warm flesh and blood once more.

"Do as I do, Dora, and Helen placed her balled hand between my shoulders and pressed heavily on the spine the whole way down, recommencing at the nape of the neck. After two or three turns, finding herself stopped by the size of what, in my figure, amounts almost to a deformity, she ceased to press, and began to examine its geography with her spread palm. Was this what she meant by the carte du pays? It seemed to tickle her fancy hugely; at length giving it a pretty hard slap, she said, —

"What a favorite you will be!"

"Nay, Helen," I replied, "even you scarcely know me yet, and the other girls, I am sure, will not view me with your partial eyes."

"Pooh! I don't mean them; they will like you well enough, I daresay. I was thinking of Martinet."

"Of her? Why?"

Then a reminiscence flashed through my mind of something I

had heard of the strict discipline of Shrewsbury House, so that I trembled and turned pale.

"Now listen to me, Dora," said Helen, "for I see you are a timid thing, and will go frightening yourself into low spirits else. Without you set fire to the chapel, or do something out of the way like that, you are as safe here as in your mother's house. Great crimes will only bring you to the "Screechery," and for less we have absolutely no punishments; no pandying, locking up, or starving to save their miserable bread and butter, as in common schools. You saw our fare last night, and it is the same all the year round. Do you believe what I say?"

"Yes, I am sure you would not deceive me; and as I am not very likely to burn a church, I shall never taste the rod, for that, I presume, is what you mean."

"H—m! I'm nae sae sure o' that. Aiblins ye may greet for it yersel."

"Me wish to be whipped! Am I mad?"

"You're ignorant, my dear. Let's change the subject. Would you like to hear about Miss De Vere?"

"What, the new girl that is expected to-day?" I heard them talking of her at tea, but either I was sleepy, or there was very little said."

"Of course there was little said with her Majesty on her throne. Did you remark a red-haired girl that sat on your left with a torn frock and a head like a poodle?"

"Oh, yes! she was so funny, she looked like a clever fool."

"Ha! ha! so she does. Well, that was Patty Wilkins, Scatterbrains, or the Wild Indian, she is mostly called. Her father, Major Wilkins, is agent to Lord Hawtry, who is Miss De Vere's uncle and part guardian, so Patty knows all about the family, and after Martinet went out she told us that magnificent young lady, Miss De Vere, was the terror of the country side; proud as Lucifer, and with such a temper there is no getting a decent maid to wait on her. She broke a rib of the last, and frightened Lady Hawtry into fits; so her Lord wrote to the Chancellor, and between them they resolved on sending her here, where she'll meet her match and more, were she twenty devils. If she is half as bad as they say, Martinet will take the change out of her the first fortnight.   Oh! that I may be there to see."

"You told me there was no secondary punishments; surely you don't mean to say that Martinet would whip a lady such as you describe Miss De Vere to be, or that her friends would suffer it to be done."

"Wouldn't she?   And what did they send her here for then? — Come in."

This last remark was addressed to Mabel Crofts, the prettiest of the parlour-maids, who, as the great bell began to toll, entered with coffee on a salver. Something in the appearance of our faces on the pillow caused her to look a note of interrogation, when Helen, flinging off the clothes ere I could catch, revealed our shiftless bodies. I squatted, blushed, and embraced my knees, while she spread her limbs wide on an imaginary Grecian cross, with an air of comic bravado.

At this display Mabel smiled, but seemed in no whit disconcerted; nor while she told her news did either of us alter her relative posture.

"Dress quickly, both," she said, "and I will show you something before breakfast. There's a two-horse van in the yard with boxes and things labelled Honble. Miss De Vere; she's to have the rooms in the east turret, where they're taking them to now. Jackson is to wait on her, and has got the keys to lay out her fallals; and that, Miss Helen, I think you'll say, is *a sicht for sai een.*"

CHAPTER V.

The Summer-house — Stories of Lives — Advent of the Hon. Miss De Vere.

AFTER breakfast Goodwin, who was anxious to reach home, took leave of me, and I charged her with a thousand loves to mama, and an assurance that I felt perfectly happy where I was;

"which, my dear, you may well be," said the kind old lady, "for, indeed, it's more like Queen Victoria's palace than a boarding school."

As there was nothing to be done that day, and no preparation needed for the morrow, we dispersed about the grounds in quest of amusement. A large party adhered to me as the new girl, and showed me les êtres, as the French call them ; I don't think we have any one word to express the ins and outs of a place. I found them a wild set, somewhat rough, but not unfriendly, except one of the bigger girls, a Miss Dickson, who contradicted and spoke to me in such a bullying way, that I got quite alarmed, till kind Helen came to the rescue, and shut her up with a snap, as Patty Wilkins said.

When we were tired of exercise we took refuge from the heat in a summer-house, which was provided with a table and abundance of rustic seats. One of the girls brought forth from a locker a tray of rusks, a basket of apples, raspberry vinegar, glasses, and a jug, which last she filled from a stream of ice-cold water that trinkled by the door.

Having done justice to this impromptu feast, more delicious, I thought, than all the luxuries of the house, we began to relate our several histories ; the prosaic did so in plain prose, the born poets added no little spice of romance. One heroine in especial, rising fifteen, had been the subject of a fatal duel, had broken off two matches, and caused a suicide and a divorce. How we all laughed ! While this was going on, Nora Blake, an Irish girl, whose curiosity to witness the new arrival was intense, had volunteered to act as scout, and now waved her handkerchief from afar. Alons ! Courons ! Suivez-moi ! And we all clambered up to a bush-clad eminence which commanded the avenue and house.

In an open barouche and four, with postillions in sky blue jackets and jockey caps sat a middle aged lady, evidently not Miss De Vere. But here she comes on horseback, followed by two grooms in dark frock coats ; she is on a milk-white Arab, with flowing mane and tail ; they on bay hunters. What a magnificent creature she is! superbly scornful, and setting her steed as if it were a part of herself. Her broad shoulders and bust were set off by the tight fitting jacket; and notwithstanding the mass of auburn hair, her aquiline nose, keen eye, and square cut chin, seemed those of a handsome man, when surmounted by the hat.

To the right of the avenue was a sunk fence in the lawn, and beyond it a gatehouse with a small sallyport, which happened at the time to be open. She turned her horse's head and bounded off, clearing the trifling obstacle without an effort, in the direction of the gate. Quick as her motions had been, the grooms were equally on the alert; one headed her by a shorter way, and ordered the gate to be shut, the other following close at her heels. Finding herself thus baffled, she led again over the ha-ha, dashed up to the hall door, and jumped down just as Lady Hawtry was about to enter the house. One of the grooms made a gesture as if to intercept her; she drew her whip, and we all thought would have struck the man; however, she only cut his horse over the nose. The frightened animal plunged and drew back, and in the confusion that ensued, Miss De Vere brushed past Lady Hawtry into the house, and — we saw her no more that day.

In about an hour the equipage was ordered round. Her ladyship came out looking infinitely relieved, and drove off, followed at a respectful distance by the grooms, one of them leading the white Arab with an empty side saddle.

CHAPTER VI.

SCHOOL ROUTINE — LECTURE OF THE IRISH PROFESSOR — WHAT MABEL CROFTS THOUGHT OF HIM.

AND how did the tigress conduct herself in the sheepfold where she was penned?"

I may say generally, that she made her appearance next day

"with us, but not of us;" she appeared to ignore our existence unless we could be of any service, when she issued her mandate curtly, and woe to the recusant. The only one she addressed willingly was Helen, who, for reasons of her own, humored her, and suppressed a conspiracy amongst us which would have brought matters to a crisis earlier.

By some means unknown, Martinet had, from the first, established such an influence over Miss De Vere, as to induce her to obey orders in a sulky indolent way. Often she would reply with abundance of insolence of tone, but never, I remarked, did she venture to exchange glances with Martinet, the glare of whose eye she shunned as the lunatic does that of the keeper. It was a terrible sight at times to watch the undercurrent of these two fierce tempers: the air was surcharged with electricity, and it was evident that the storm, when it did burst, would be a fearful one.

Revenons à nos moutons; and dear Jacintha, bear with me if I seem to linger on the sunny side of Shrewsbury House. You will have action enough presently, and I fear you will feel shocked at the revelations I must make. Remember that you sought them, and that, under circumstances certainly unprecedented, I am scarcely to be blamed if my character, or at least my inclinations, received a marked bias.

This was the daily habit of our lives. We rose at a quarter before six, and had tea or coffee according to choice, each pair of girls being served in their own room. At half-past six the whole household assembled in the hall, which had two fire-places, always lighted in winter. Here prayers were read by the housekeeper, Mrs. Giles, a clergyman's widow, and pious in her way. From the hall the pupils passed to morning class.

The main school-room was remarkable for size and elegance of fittings; the desks and benches were of carved oak, the latter had fixed cushions covered with green morocco leather. There were little pulpits for the teachers, and about the centre of the room a railed daïs, raised by three steps from the level of the floor. Here Martinet sat enthroned, commanding a view of all her subjects. Her knowledge, both classical and scientific, was such that she could be referred to in all difficulties, but her specialty was rather to guide and superintend than to teach. In case of any misdemeanor during school hours, the monitress of the class where it occurred would make her report: the delinquent would then have to mount the daïs, always a trying ordeal, though the worst that could happen there was a verbal reprimand more or less severe. There was, indeed, the "bill," but of that further on.

At nine o'clock we had a substantial breakfast á la fourchette, and much in the French style, save that café au lait or other harmless drinks were substituted for wine. Class again from half-past ten to twelve. There was no regular luncheon, but all who chose might repair for sandwiches or other dainties to Mrs. Giles. At four or five o'clock, according to the season, we sat down to a sumptuous dinner, whereat costly wines were served in moderation, enough to exhilarate, but no more. At eight there was the tea already mentioned, than one hour of preparation in the school-room for the morrow's work. At half-past ten all must be in bed and every light extinguished.

Thus you see we had scarce more than four hours of actual study in the day; but there were extra classes for drawing, music, dancing, and calisthenics, besides occasional lectures from men of talent in various branches of knowledge, each study having its appropriate room fitted with scientific apparatus, diagrams and the like. The earliest of these lectures I remember as having been peculiarly interesting. The celebrated Professor H—— had been engaged to give us a series of lectures on astronomy and geology, and now introduced both subjects in a joint and general manner.

It was like a theatre, for we occupied graduated benches rising half-way up the room. On the opposite wall were representations of our earth, connected with the sun and other planetary bodies by lines figured with high numbers indicating distances.

In front and a little to one side stood the lecturer, pointing

with a pole.   He was a handsome florid man, not above thirty
years of age, and with a splendid figure.   His look was grave,
nor was there the slightest impropriety in anything he said ; for
all that, his large earnest eyes were making love, and his tones
conveyed a continuous compliment.   Those tones were rich and
racy, and he did not make the slightest effort to disguise his
nationality.

Speaking of the wonders of sidereal motion and its difficulty
of appreciation by the uneducated, he said something to the following effect : —"I remember my poor father, a worthy clergyman in the West of Ireland, once telling his labourers that the
sun was a million times larger than the earth, and that the earth
itself was spinning round one thousand miles in one direction,
and flying round sixty-eight thousand miles an hour in another.
I suppose he intended to have explained farther, but something
called him away at the moment, and his hearers were left under
the shock of the first announcement.   One of them stood with
his mouth wide open, and evident signs of blank dismay in his
countenance.   Another, he was reckoned the Solomon of the
party, says to him : — ' Sorra word o' truth in it, ye big bost-
hoon, only lies the master was tellin' ye, to divert himself with
yer ignorance.' "

At this, his only lapse into levity, we all tittered, save Martinet ; her grave looks chilled him for a time, but could not
quench the inborn eloquence of the man when he warmed into
his favorite theme, geology.   The present seemed to drop from
us as naught, whilst he rolled us back with him for countless
centuries, describing the probable formation of the earth's crust,
and the pre-adamite zoology, with its mystic nomenclature of
mastodon and icthyosaurus.

"What an awfully sublime picture," he said, "arises in the
mind's eye at the thought of a world of mist and swamp roamed
over by these huge leviathans ; where no voice of man broke
the perpetual silence, and the vegetation, uncared for, grew
rank and wild till it rotted in despair ! . . . . . And in the upper
portion of this upper crust alone are found the traces of the

monarch *Man*. Yet to us what long ages seem to have elapsed since the commencement of his dynasty! The last and greatest of modern poets, contrasting the brevity of Man's days with the duration of his words, writes thus: —

> ' Frail Man! when paper, even a rag like this,
>   Survives himself, his tomb and all that's his,
>   And when his bones are dust, his grave a blank,
>   His station, generation, even his nation
> Become as things of nothing, save to rank
>   In chronological commemoration ;
> Some dull manuscript oblivion long has sank,
>   On graven stone found in a barrack's station
> In digging the foundation of a closet,
> Shall turn his name up as a rare deposit!' "

I have not done justice to H——'s words : the poet's (Byron's I believe, though I do not remember where the lines occur), I wrote down at the time; but here again I am powerless to give the thrilling tones that ravished the ears of the audience. Even Martinet herself seemed struck, and scarcely quarrelled with our breach of conventional rule by a round of hand-clappings.

When the lecturer took his leave, he announced his wish to go by the orchard to the village; Mabel Crofts was accordingly sent to show him the path and unlock the postern. When she returned amongst us girls, her cheeks redder than usual and her eyes dancing with merriment, we asked her what she thought of the professor.

"A be-yewtiful man, ladies, and don't smoke."

"How do you know that?"

"I should know if he did."

Then she added sententiously — "Oh! that a man should put an enemy into his mouth to steal away his — kisses!"

CHAPTER VII.

JACKY IN THE APPLE-TREE — THE SONG OF THE SIREN — THE SPY.

NEXT to Helen Macgregor my prime favorite was Mabel. Though ostensibly only a parlor-maid, the pretty creature was so engaging and ladylike in manner, that Martinet, who, I told you, was an admirer of beauty in her own sex, did not object to her joining us whenever she was at leisure in our hours of recreation. Mabel's father, a substantial yeoman, would have kept her to home, but she was restless and wished to adopt the profession of an actress. To compromise matters she had been placed with a musical lady in our neighbourhood, who taught her singing and other accomplishments. While she was there she heard of a place vacant at Shrewsbury House, and the name of that fashionable establishment, with its reputation for choice of beauties only, tempted her to enter it even in a menial capacity.

Mabel was a rake at heart, with the drollest air of mock modesty, a regular Sainte Nitouche, if ever there was one : indeed her chief attraction lay in her French *malice*, differing, you know, from the English article of the same name. I cannot give you a better idea of her than by describing a transaction which took place about ten days after Miss De Vere's arrival; a relation of this, moreover, will be found necessary to the elucidation of my story.

Mabel had been sent on commission to the village, and I, having stolen a duplicate pass-key, strolled out through the orchard to meet her on her return. It was but a trifling peccadillo, yet the shadow of a coming event seemed to forewarn me. I hesitated. Would it have been better if I had gone back ? I scarce know ; probably it would have come to the same thing in the end.

There is Mabel climbing the stile. An artist would have chosen that moment to sketch her light figure standing in bold relief against the azure back-ground. The day being warm, I waited in the shade till she joined me, when we both sat down on a sofa of nature's providing to take breath and enjoy the sights and sounds around us.

We were just entering into conversation when we perceived two round ruddy cheeks, and a pair of blue eyes directed at us from an adjoining thicket; these belonged to the gardener's grandson, a flaxen-haired laddy, twelve years old perhaps, and well grown, but quite a simpleton. Mabel beckoned to him, and he approached with a broad grin very slowly.

"Don't be afraid, Jacky," said she, "we ain't going to eat you. Can you climb a tree? See those rosy apples over my head, we should like some of them."

He swarmed up the tree with the agility of a monkey and soon reached the fruit, though not without an accident: in spreading wide his legs a crack was heard; as he presented the apples he became aware of the nature and extent of the damage, and began to whimper.

"They're my best, and I warn't to put em on but o' Sundays. Och! Granny 'll leather me."

"Don't cry, child," said Mabel, drawing out her housewife, "here, take them off, and I'll set them to rights for you."

He complied without a moment's hesitation and handed her the corduroys. Jacky was now standing between us, and his legs were just over my hand; I could not resist the temptation to slip it up between them. He did not resent the liberty, but still kept his round eyes fixed on Mabel, who asked me with a wink what it felt like.

"Like your nipple," I replied, "only smaller."

"Small, is it?"

> "Ah! little things bring back to me
> The thought of bygone hours."

"Never mind, we'll enlarge its dimensions presently. Here," drawing the last stitch, "here they are, Jacky, but before you put them on, would you like to stretch on my lap while I sing a song for you?"

"Oh, yes! miss, please!"

Mabel settled her shoulders against the bank, tucked up the front of her smart dress, and joining her feet, let her knees down at either side under her scarlet petticoat. She then thrust the tails of Jacky's shirt under his waistcoat, laid him face upwards on her lap, and commenced her song piano et con amore.

OVERTURE.

"Lullaby, Baby, on the tree top,
 When the wind blows the cradle will rock.
 If the bough breaks, the cradle will fall,
 Down will come Baby, cradle and all."

Mabel's voice was a sweet one, and sounded all the sweeter for its tone of mockery. How pretty they both looked! he gazing up flushed and delighted, she bending till the brown curls fanned his cheek. One arm supported his neck, the hand hidden in his bosom. With the right which was next to me, she marked time as on an instrument.

"Ah! the rogue wants me to begin."

SONG AND RECITATIVE OF ACTION.

"Here we go up-up-up,
 Here we go down, down, downy,
 Here we go backwards and forwards —
   Come o'er the heather
   We'll trip together
 All in the morning early;
 heed neither father, nor mother, nor brother —
 The Campbells are coming, hurra! hurra!
 The Campbells are coming, hurra! —
   There was a little Jack,
   And his breeches had a crack,
 And his bullets were made of —
   Hey this! What's that?
 This is the lass that was left forlorn,
 That milked the cow with the crumplety horn,
   That toss'd the dog,
   That worried the cat,
   That killed the rat,
   That ate the malt
 That lay in the — Cock that Jack kilt!"

The gipsy must have been born for the stage. Throughout her varied medley her voice never faltered, nor did her fingers lose the time.   The pause at "Hey this! What's that!" she made use of to change the stops of her instrument; then voice and hand were off again at racing speed, and when she reached the finale, she tossed the urchin upwards in her lap, who glued his lips to hers, and thrust his hand deep into her bosom.

By this time Mabel and I were both on fire, and there is no saying what further improprieties might have been committed, had we not been warned by a cry from the boy.   Looking up hastily, we were aware of the figure of Steinkopf gliding off in the distance.

Jacky, more alarmed than either of us, had already decamped with his breeches on his arm, and we returned, considerably sobered to the school-house.

End of Part First of Revelations of Shrewsbury House.

PEN PICTURES.

No. IV.

THE SCREECHERY.

The Screechery! a name of dire import,
There the delinquent Dora must resort.
As only females enter the Locked Room,
Leave is allowed to pencil and to plume.

The startled eye, retreating from the block,
Wanders around to find recurring shock.
Patty, "balloon'd," with rotatory hand,
Nurses her rear in "sobbing saraband."
How sore it is, her writhen features show,
Is it thro' modesty she hides it? No.
Did not the dusting her discretion blunt,
She would not show us her uncovered front.
Whatever else escape us, we espy
The rainbow tints that circle the right thigh.

Helen, just whipt, in Nature's lilies dight,
Catches a shift-sleeve in her elbow's bight;
The falling shroud, arrested but by half,
Displays the further stocking to the calf.
Erect and blooming, not a sign of fear,
She looks a — How do you like it?" at *De Vere.*

She, haught of port, in utmost mode equipt,
Lingers awhile, to see the last one whipt.

A ward in Chancery, and nobly born,
She laughs scholastic discipline to scorn,
Never imagining *her* sacred form
Could be exposed to ignominious storm.

While *Martinet*, prolonging pleasant tryst,
Adjusts the glittering bracelet on her wrist,
The cruel *Renardeau* impatient bends,
Poising the weapon on her finger ends.

Dora, pinn'd up, and forced upon her knees,
Shrinks from the wanton wooing of the breeze;
Vain every effort to elude the smart
By muscular contraction of the part.
Armstrong and *Steinkopf* of the inky dress
Grapple her arms and on her shoulders press.

And still no agony — no fierce assault!

Will she relent, and pardon a first fault?

Turning with half a hope, poor Dora knows
What means *the* look — the harbinger of woes.

REVELATIONS OF SHREWSBURY HOUSE.

PART SECOND.

CHAPTER VIII.

RETRIBUTION COMMENCES — OUTBREAK OF MISS DEVERE — DORA'S
DREAM — SHE IS COMFORTED BY HELEN.

BEFORE coming in sight of the windows, Mabel and I kissed
each other with sad hearts.

"Do you think she 'll tell, Mabel?"

"Think! I 'm sure of it. You will be taken to the locked
room to-morrow, and I that would give my eyes to see it, will be
sent away just as I was beginning to love all here. Ah, me! I
wish I was a lady to be whipped like one of you. I would not
mind the pain a bit."

My feelings, already excited, were destined to encounter a
fresh shock, for on mounting the stairs, I found a group of girls
in the gallery looking with frightened faces toward the east turret where loud cries and screams were heard. Presently the
door flew open, and Jackson, one of the housemaids, fled, pursued by Miss De Vere, cutting her with a horsewhip over the
bare neck and arms.

"Do, you jade," she bellowed, her voice being heard above
the cries, "do, and tell her, if she gives me another of her looks,
I 'll serve her with the same sauce."

I did not wait to learn the issue, but retreated to our room.
Where was Helen? Alas! Helen was on a two days' visit to
friends passing through Shrewsbury, and would not be back till

late this night, possibly not till the next, when all would be over. I tried to fix my attention on lessons, but I could not sit at ease, and my eyes filled constantly with tears. I cried till the tea bell rang, when I washed my face and crept down. Martinet was there, looking radiant; and to my surprise she addressed a civil remark to Miss De Vere, who sat swelling with gratified malice, and scarce vouchsafed an answer. If she were forgiven, there might be hope for me. I caught Martinet's eye; she smiled more than ever, but the undefinable expression was distinctly visible; it boded no good when seen for the first time on her face.

Ten o'clock. No use in sitting up for Helen. I should only fall asleep in my chair, and may as well do so in bed. I lay there pondering on Martinet's expression, which grew ever darker and more weird, till her features changed to those of the Autocrat of all the Russias. He frowned. I had committed some inexpiable offence connected with an apple, and was dragged underground to a loathsome vault, where stony-visaged senators pronounced my doom —

DEATH BY THE LASH!

Legions of armed men surrounded me and formed a square. Within it were a post with dangling cords, a coffin, and a band of executioners, grim in beard and sheepskin, flourishing terrific knouts. One of them sprang towards me, tore off my clothes, and shouted in my ear —

"Wake, Dora, wake!"

O blessed sight! It's Helen in her night-shift shaking me by the arm.

"Why, child, how you tremble, and what set you thinking of the knout? Something mnst have happened. Come into my bed and tell me all about it."

I did so, resting my head on her warm bosom. As I narrated the adventure in the orchard, and Mabel's song, I could feel her shake with suppressed laughter. At the horsewhipping, which she made me tell twice over, she clapped her hands with glee.

"Now listen, Dora. You will be whipped as sure as fate to-morrow at twelve, but mark my words, so will she. Would it be any comfort to you if I were there to?"

"Yes, surely, the greatest comfort. But would Martinet allow it?"

"Not for nothing, truly. I'll be there, nevertheless. Leave that to me."

"And Mabel will be turned off. Poor Mabel! She said she wished she could be whipped like one of us."

"Did she so? Then I think I can manage that too. Yewhaw! It's very late, Dozy, let's go to sleep now."

Brighter thoughts came with the dawn. Why had I been so ridiculously cast down overnight? While it was yet six hours off, I even felt that I could face the "Screechery" with brave Helen by my side. However bad, it cannot be more than a few moments' pain, and then I should not be the only one. It was evident that this would be a day of intense excitement. The thought of my own share of the drama to be enacted at twelve did not so overwhelm me but that I was able to note with interest the circumstances of the day.

Helen was already up, and commencing her toilet.

"Why, Helen," I exclaimed, "what a ridiculous shift! it is sizes too large, and won't stay on without it's held."

"The stays hold it, you see."

"But why wear it? You have plenty there the right size."

"Qui vivra verra," she replied.

At the quarter precisely our rolls and coffee were brought in, but not by Mabel.

"Why, Betty," said Helen, "what brought *you* here?"

"You cùm late last night," Miss, but surely Miss Doveton told you summat. Mabel's been locked up by the Missis herself. She's crying, poor soul, and says she's to leave to-morrow, but won't tell for why; leastways she says that you, Miss Doveton, knows. Then Jackson should ha' waited on you, not me: but lor sake, miss, if you only seen her neck and arms after the weltin' she got from that she devil, Miss De Vere; and all for noth-

ink at all, only advising her to mind what the missis said. With
that she out with the riding whip she hid when the horses was
took from her, and fell on her, which it's my belief she'd ha'
murthered her on the spot, only Jackson she slep into the Jar-
min woman's room and bolted the door."

"So I was told. I suspect she'll hear more of that by-and-by.
Meanwhile do you think I could manage to speak to Mabel?"

"Yes, Miss Helen, I know you can. The key of my room fits
her's, which I've been into her myself." In about five minutes
Helen returned, saying —

"It's all right with Mabel, she won't have to leave this time."

"How ever did you manage it so soon?"

"I have not managed it yet; I've only put her up to a dodge.
No doubt she'll catch it tight, but so will you, and get your
allowance first; so now, you miserable sinner, come down to
prayers."

Prayers, morning class, and breakfast passed much as usual,
save that there was a general feeling of nervousness, and we all
remarked the absence of Miss De Vere. As we were leaving
the breakfast for the school-room Renardeau entered. I lingered
near the door and heard Martinet ask if she had sent up Miss
De Vere's breakfast, to which the Frenchwoman made this ominous reply : —

"Je lui servis moi-même, madame, afin de voir quelle mine
ait sou altesse royale. Elle est en grande tenue, ce qui nous
embarrassera sans doute, mais enfin, vous le voulez. Ainsi,
j'avais dit d'abord que vous le seriez aussi, qu'une de nos belles
devait avoir le fouet pour faire peur aux autres, et qu'il fallait
se bien mettre pour *assister* aux grand spectacles."

And now, relying on the implied promise of secrecy, I will
take my Jacintha by the hand, *and Jacintha only*, bring her into
the school-room first, and from thence conduct her to the "locked
chamber," where under the specious name of discipline vile passions were let loose, and deeds were done, the records of which
must be seen by no eyes but hers and mine.

CHAPTER IX.

THE SCHOOL-ROOM — THE BILL — "THE SCREECHERY" — EXPERI-
ENCES OF PATTY, HELEN, AND DORA — THE HONORABLE JANE
CAROLINE FINDS THE LORD CHANCELLOR AGAINST HER.

ELEVEN o'clock had just struck, bringing with it the dismal
images connected with the one stroke more. To banish these I
endeavored to fix my thoughts on passing events.

Our form had been examined in English history by Miss
Armstrong, who is slowly passing in front, her back towards us,
questioning the opposing form on the events of a certain reign.
The cat meanwhile has crept in, and Patty Wilkins, ever in
mischief, has fastened her garter to its tail. Miss Armstrong is
right in front, and from her pocket depends a ball of tape.
Another girl makes a sign and foolish Patty unites the two
strings. Miss Armstrong moves, and Pussy, feeling her tail
twitched, bounds off, the ball gets entangled in the pocket, the
knots are securely tied, and a scene of indescribable confusion,
of spitting, shrieks, and laughter ensues.

Martinet is up, and demands with flashing eyes : — "Qui est
ce qui l'faite ? "

Good-humored Armstrong, I think, would have screened her,
but the monitress does her duty and names the delinquent.

"Qu' elle monte ! "

This at least I had escaped, for my offence was committed out of
school. Poor Patty ! despite her red hair and freckles, she looked
quite pretty with her wild frightened face and wonderfully fair
skin.   There she stands, the observed of all observers, shifting
uneasily from foot to foot, and tying nervous knots on her pock-
et-handkerchief. Martinet's face is buried in her desk, the lid
of which trembles above it. While the culprit's fate thus hangs
in the balance, Renardeau, armed with a stiletto looking pen,
springs upon the stage and tears off Patty's jacket, as though
about to stab her. The Frenchwoman had cause for wrath, for
the rough rape revealed the absence of a vest, a soiled chemise,
and back that invited beating.

"Regardez donc, Madame! quelle mise, au plutôt, quel manque de mise! Vingt fois que je lui ai parlé. C'est affreux!"

"Tiens," cries Martinet, "attens que je cherche. J'eus besoin d'une autre, mais je crois que nous l'ayous attrapée. Un—deux—ha! c'est ça—Voilà!"

She let the lid down with a bang, and showed the shivering Patty a book wherein her own name figured conspicuously. Taking the pen from Renardeau, Martinet reinscribed Miss Wilkins's name, adding date and particulars.

"Conduite scandaleuse, troisième fois; punie ilya un mois, une fois pardonnée.

"Couvrez vous, mademoiselle ; ce n'est pas ici le lieu ni l'endroit ; on vous fera faire voir ailleurs. Chut! Point de repousé. *Al-lez!*"

Patty then crept back amongst us, and business was resumed. In due time — how long it seemed to me! — the classes were dismissed, and with them vanished my last hope, as I saw the monitress interpose her person between me and the door. Laying a hand on each, she said : —

"Doveton and Wilkins are to stay."

Helen had lingered behind the rest ; she now sprang forward and asked in a loud voice : —

"Dora Doveton! what for?"

"That, Miss Macgregor, can be no business of yours," replied Martinet; "suffice it to say that Miss Steinkopf—"

"Steinkopf is a liar and a spy, but she shall not always escape."

So saying, the bold girl hurled an inkstand with unerring aim at Steinkopf's dress, which was utterly destroyed.

"Verdammter Hurenbalg, diess, sollt ihr reun!"

The enraged German, springing forward, was arrested by Martinet, who, strange to say, looked approvingly at Helen.

"Calm yourself, Miss Steinkopf, remember in whose presence you are, and don't use such vulgar language. Depend upon it, full justice shall be done. Add Miss Macgregor's name to the bill 'for insolence to *me;*' your loss shall be made good."

She passed out, and the entry being made, we were surrounded by a group consisting of Renardeau, Steinkopf, Armstrong, and Atkinson, the monitress of the class in which Patty and I then were. Atkinson was a sullen, beetle-browed young woman, twenty years of age, and next to Armstrong the strongest in the school. Resistance would have been vain; Helen evidently had no thought of such, for she led the way with a defiant air; I followed close, and Patty, half giggling, half crying, was shoved along in our rear.

As we passed in procession along the inhabited parts of the house, we were peeped at from behind doors and corners by faces indicative of various emotions; and I had the mortification to find that our disgrace was no secret even to the domestics, for one of these made a mocking gesture as of whipping with her duster, to which Patty Wilkins responded in her silly way, by clapping both hands to her stern with a grimace of agony that threw the housemaids into fits of laughter.

We now came to a door, the subject of dread and speculation to all the uninitiated. When this door was locked behind us, the scene was a dismal one; the shutters of all the windows were closed, and the light that struggled through the chinks left the shapes of things almost to conjecture.

We mounted a creaking staircase; gallery after gallery, flight after flight was passed, and still we ascended till the brain grew dizzy at the thought of the height and isolation. At length we reached a massive iron-sheathed door, over the portal of which might have been inscribed Dante's —

"LASCIATE OGNI SPERANZA ! "

This door never opened but for punishment. The guard surrounded us here and thrust us in; the heavy bolt crashed back, the door was locked, and the key consigned to Renardeau's pocket.

It was a loft of apparently interminable length, where some half a century before the then inhabitants had stored their used-up furniture. The roof sloped nearly to the floor, and was partially divided by uprights supporting the rafters. In each compartment was a trap window; the corners, however, were obscure, and in them the old upholstery and dresses looked spectral.

On our arrival, Martinet, who must have entered by another door, was already there, and conversing with Miss De Vere. Martinet wore a skirt of rich moire, that gave additional breadth to the lower part of her person; the body, which would have cramped the play of her terrible arms, was absent, her bust being covered only by a white linen jacket with loose sleeves. De Vere was in full dress, and brilliantly handsome; a look of pleased excitement having replaced the habitual scowl on her haughty brow. Despite Helen's assurance, I could not believe that she was there otherwise than as a spectatress of our punishment. But my own affairs were too pressing to allow me to bestow much thought on those of others.

Which of our names will be called first?

That matter was apparently decided by an accident. Behind Martinet and De Vere was some dread object, the outlines of which I could scarce sketch. Patty Wilkins sees it and is about to bolt, but is collared by the vindictive Frenchwoman. Renardeau looks to Martinet, who nods approval, and the blundering "Wild Indian" is dragged up as first victim.

Finding no attention paid to me, I slipped into the next compartment, when feeling faint, I opened the skylight and looked out. Then, indeed, I saw that this was

> "————— a place of punishment
> Whence never shriek so loud was sent,
> Could reach the *lower* air."

The old building was completely detached from the new, which it overtopped by many feet; the windows where we were looked upon the rear. Down — fathoms deep below — was the gloomy lake, the orchard on the far shore so distant that the shapes of the trees could scarcely be distinguished.

Oh! for the wings of a bird to flee from the stern tones pronouncing doom so near me! The conclusion of the sentence was distinctly audible — "I had hoped that the last lesson would have sufficed; this time you shall feel the full weight of my arm. Strip her!"

To this succeeded a loud sound of sobs and scuffling — then a momentary silence — then burst forth such shrieks and yells as showed the need there was of isolation, and the appropriateness of the term "Screechery."

Even in cases of painful accident, where all are eager to relieve, how appalling are reiterated cries! Now, the malignity seemed diabolical that could persist for moments together in the infliction of such mortal agony. I thrust my fingers in my ears; I stamped to drown the sound, and finally, I believe, roared in chorus.

The din has ceased at length. It is Helen's turn now, and I must needs listen.

"Again, Miss Macgregor, I find you subjecting yourself to the ignominious punishment of the rod; you, who from your age and standing in the school, should set an example. But where is her companion? She must witness her punishment."

"Doveton! Dora! Dora Doveton!"

I tried to fancy it was some other name they called, then hearing rushing footsteps, slunk into a dark corner. The search was ineffectual for some time, till the dust it raised, obliging me to sneeze, Renardeau pounced like cat on mouse on me: —

> "Ah! te voilà en cachette, ça n'ira pas. Viens voir
> Comment tu l'aimeras; après quoi nous verrons un peu
> Cette ad mi *rable* derrière à la peau veloutée."

With these words she dragged me into the presence, and there held me in her iron grasp by the arm, which it pained exceedingly.

Unable any longer, ostrich like, to conceal my head, I looked up and beheld a scene —

But let me first describe one of a similar nature, but very different complexion.

The summer after you left, while sharing with your sisters the instructions of Miss Prim, I had witnessed the administration of the birch by that most modest and good-humored of young ladies. Prize medallist of her college, learned and accomplished, the only objection to her as a governess was her youth, which might detract from her authority over her pupils. To obviate this, she had your mama's commands to punish freely, and for the sake of example, always in our presence. When resort to the rod became inevitable, Prim, blushing to the roots of her blonde hair, would retire with the culprit to a remote corner of the school-room, where, after a moment of unseen preliminaries, she would sit down facing the wall, the skirts of her book muslin fantailed round her waist, and her fat shoulders so square to the spectators that little of the other party to the transaction was visible but a flushed face and slippers in convulsions. Among so many there were various degrees of reluctance or *otherwise*. Philly, in especial, would cry, ' harder yet,' and drub the ankles and bump upon the lap, till Prim, in self-defence, was obliged to put forth the full force of her well-rounded arm. As a guest I was not subjected to this dicipline, which did not seem to me to be very formidable. We can judge of the unseen only by the seen, and on this model I had formed my notions of school punishment. Brought for the first time face to face with the naked facts of the Screechery, I felt a blending of awe, astonishment, and disgust, the latter feeling so powerful as almost to turn my stomoch.

I shall now, as far as I dare, describe what I saw.

The object that had scared Patty proved to be a heavy stool, rivited, I believe, to the floor, with an upright front, in shape somewhat like an executioner's block, whereon the culprit knelt low and erect to receive the discipline. This block was covered with black cloth, and rested on a carpet of the same under the sky-light, so that the flesh-tints exposed on it, contrasting with the sombre ground, came out with photographic distinctness. The floor around was strewed with the fragments of a broken rod; Patty, her petticoats still pinned about her neck, was

dancing a sort of sobsaraband which left the spectator in no
doubt as to the cause of her gyrations.   On the block knelt
Helen, my own Helen, in the hands of the Philistines.

Stays being inadmissible in the supreme moment, hers had
been removed and lay upon a pile of her upper clothing. Wanting this support, the over-wide chemise had dropped to the
middle of her back, where being met by the upturned tail and
twisted into a rope, it formed a belt of white sufficient to show
that she *had been* covered.   At either side of the block and a
little to the rear stood Armstrong and Atchinson, Steinkopf
having been made by Martinet to yield her place to the latter
in the present instance. These two held the rope lightly, rather
to support it than to confine the culprit, whose arms they left
free, with a dependence on her pluck which was not belied by
her looks, for her cheeks blazed, her breasts heaved, and her
eyes shone like carbuncles with *the* expression.

On Martinet I dared not look ; being, however, aware of the
motion of her arm, I turned aside my head and covered it with
my apron.

I said that Patty's screams alarmed me, but I was even more
horrified at the stoic silence which allowed every lash of the
many-twigged rod to be heard cutting deep into the flesh with
monotonous rhythm, interrupted only by occasional rasps against
the block or the dress of the assistants.

There is a pause at last — my head reels, for my own turn
will come next — nay, my own turn *is come !*

"Once more I order you to come here and stand before me."

I was dropping to the floor, when Renardeau caught me by
the neck and thrust under my nose a bottle of some pungent
essence which instantly revived me.

"Va qu'elle te chatouille !" she hissed into my ear, giving me
a shove to hasten my movements.

Martinet's dreaded voice could indeed make me stand trembling before her, but no power could have induced me to look her
in the face then.   Even her shining shoes on which my eyes
rested, seemed replete with menace.

"Dora Doveton."

Her tones were preternaturally calm, like the senators in my dream, and frightened me far more than angry scolding.

"Scarce ten days arrived here, you find your way already to the whipping-room. And on what charge? For participation in a crime so wicked and at the same time so disgustingly obscene, I cannot pollute the ears of those present by even hinting at its nature. Such deeds, though nameless, require public and exemplary chastisement. It is now my painful duty to see if I cannot scourge that demon out of you. — Fetch two of the No. 6 rods, and unlace her, if necessary."

Renardeau darted her hand beneath my clothes and reported that I wore no stays. Nor do I now; my waist is naturally small, and a little stiffening in the body of the dress suffices to keep my breasts in order.

Steinkopf, who had resumed her place, and Armstrong, then laid hold of me, and despite my prayers and tears, while one held my hands above my head, the other opened my dress behind, and stripped off skirt, petticoats, and drawers; then with one shameless drag she furled up my shift in front and rear, and pinned it over my shoulders.

The next moment I was forced upon my knees on the block, with four hands grasping my arms and pressing my neck down. The breeze from the sky-light fanned my back, and I felt that the eyes of all present were rivited on my naked person. Could it be that I was thus subjected to such indignity? Though my arms were squeezed, I felt it not; all my sensation seemed to have retreated to another quarter. My skin is so tender that even when bathing I tremble to expose it, and here was I fixed as in a vice, with nothing intervening between that thin skin and the murderous implements behind me.

A pause, it seemed to me an hour long, ensued, till my spine grew cold as ice twixt fear and waiting. Something had rattled on the floor, but the sound had died away, and still the expected blow came not. I looked round with half a hope. Martinet was leisurely re-adjusting a bracelet on her rod arm, her eyes the while devouring my form with a wild impassioned gaze like a lover's.

Can she be relenting?

Alas! the brows contract —
the grasps of the holders tighten on my arms, —

Whir—r—r *Whisp!*

"Yah! Yeou! Yeoiks!"

Oh! the unspeakable agony of that first murderous lash! Legions of scorpions fastened on my flesh and dug their fangs into my vitals. Vainly I hung back and screwed my front against the block, the rear would not recede; I could only diminish its width by muscular contraction.

Whir-r *Whisp!* Whir-r *Whisp!* Whir-r *Whisp!*

Nature cannot endure the pain; I struggle to my feet, receiving a fifth rasper in the act, and my shrieks rival the loudest howls of Patty.

This was the "whipping proper," a few strokes more of which would probably have killed or maddened.

The two strong women soon resumed their clutch and dragged me to my bearings on the whipping stool — less reluctantly — for already the charm had worked; the mere act of rising seemed to have brought relief, and a change next to miraculous took place in all my thoughts and feelings. I noted the impressions shortly after they occurred, and shall endeavor to describe them.

Fear and shame were both gone: it was as though I was surrendering my person to the embraces of a man whom I so loved I would anticipate his wildest desires. But no man was in my thoughts; Martinet was the object of my adoration, and I felt *through the rod* that I shared her passions. The rapport, as the magnitisers have it, was so strong that I could divine her thoughts; had she wished me to turn my person full front to her stripes, I should have fought and struggled to obey her. Then, too, there was a thrill in a certain part, I knew magnetically, of both our persons, which every fresh lash kept on increasing. The added pang unlocked new floods of bliss, till it was impossible to tell in my case whether the ecstasy was most of pain or pleasure. When the rods were changed, I continued to jump and shout, for she liked that, but—believe me or not—I saw my nakedness with her eyes, and exulted in the lascivious joy that whipping me afforded her. This state would have continued as long as my strength, for I had no power to quit the spot till *my other self* willed it.

The punishment over, I broke from the assistants, and from Atkinson, who, crinoline on arm, would have acted as lady's maid, and rushed towards Martinet, intending, I believe, to throw myself at her feet, when my course was forcibly arrested by Helen. With a whispered *Steady!* she unpinned my shift, and directed my attention to the last act in this day's drama, which was now commencing.

Miss De Vere had watched the various whippings with a mixed expression in which scorn predominated. Finding no more victims coming forward for her amusement, she was about to withdraw, desiring the door to be opened for her, when she was stopped by a glance from Martinet, whose eye, when she so willed, did really possess the power which fable attributes to the basilisk.

"Hold, Miss De Vere; you have seen the punishment of those less guilty than yourself. Think you that *my* servants are to be lashed like dogs, and *my* authority set at naught with impunity? *No.* Your turn is now come, and all here whom you have daily insulted shall witness your humiliation."

"*Me!* audacious woman, have you taken leave of your senses? But, tut! I am a ward, and the protection of the Chancellor places me beyond the reach of your insolent menace."

"You are in *my* court now, where the law has sent you: behold what it ordains for one of your insolent temper."

She drew a paper from her bosom, struck it open with the disengaged hand, and read as follows:—

"I certify that my niece, the Hon. Jane Caroline De Vere,
"a ward in Chancery, and under age, by the joint authori-
"ty of the Lord Chancellor, and of myself, has been placed
"in charge of Mrs. Constance Martinet, of Shrewsbury

"House, for educational purposes. The said Miss De Vere
"being of a headstrong and unruly temper, and at times
"dangerously violent, I her uncle and natural guardian,
"acting under the advice of the Chancellor aforesaid, do
"hereby authorize and empower the said Constance Marti-
"net to use all such means of coercion and punishment as
"she shall think fit, including corporeal punishment with
"rod or cane — to be inflicted on the body of the said Jane
"Caroline De Vere. And from all damage or accident re-
"sulting from the free use of such lawful instruments, I
"hereby absolve Mrs. Martinet and hold her harmless."
    (Signed)   "HAWTRY."

During the reading of this death-warrant to her dignity we
all watched the features of the haughty patrician. Her expression was actually demoniacal, even the basilisk eye could no
longer restrain her. She gave a yell of rage and sprang forward
in act to strike, when all present, Martinet excepted, fell upon
and clung to her. Her strength was prodigious ; she swayed
the whole body of us to and fro, inflicting damaging bruises with
her knees and elbows, and could she have freed her hands from
Armstrong and Steinkopf's grasp, our lives, I am sure, would
have been in danger.

When the odds of seven to one had exhausted her powers,
Martinet directed us to a bedstead in the next compartment ; it
was covered with a mattress only, and its upper posts were gar-
nished with stout cords. Upon this we flung her, not without
difficulty, and while Renardeau sat upon her back her wrists
were bound to the posts with double knots, but her tremendous
legs were still at liberty. It was a service of real danger to approach them, and all hung back   Then Helen and I looked at
each other, for I that am generally such a coward felt brave
now. We watched our opportunity, pinned each an ankle and
dragged it to the ground, on which we dropped in a sitting
posture.

The next thing was to strip her — but how was that to be
effected? Her corsage reached so low that it would have inter-

fered with the free action of the rod, and to release her arms
would have been madness. Renardeau, who had been an out-
sider in the fight, was here in her element, and solved the riddle
in a moment. She first undid the skirts, all of which were accessible from behind, and drew them down to her heels, over
which we passed them, others assisting us. The Frenchwoman
(it was said she had been a dress-maker) took a pair of scissors
from her pocket, and with a few dexterous snips disengaged the
whalebone from the corset, cut ruthlessly through the rich silk,
and performed the like operation on the stays, slitting up half
a dozen of the laces.

Having thus prepared the way, she uncovered calves a porter
might have envied, then lifting the linen inch by inch, revealed
to those behind the whole of a situpon of prodigious size, and to
Helen and myself in our lowly posture more, probably, than
was visible to the general spectator. The palms of Renardeau's
hands were evidently itching, but she dared not interfere between the tigress and her prey.

"N'est-ce pas coco," she observed, "que de voir la fouetteuse
fouettée ?"

Martinet meanwhile had taken off her loose morning wrapper,
and armed herself with a rod, formed, not of canes and cuttings
like the rest, but of stout birch stems with innumerable branches,
like a tree in miniature.

With this weapon in her hand, how terrible she appeared!
Juno, deprived of the apple might have looked like her. Her
splendid arms and neck were bare, her cheeks flamed, her huge
breasts were heaving. Speech was too weak, the graces of
birching were ignored, nothing short of savage *beating* could
satisfy her present need of vengeance.

Two of the heaviest of the assistants sat upon the victim's
shoulders. I drew aside from the sweep of that terrific rod that
tore through the air with the whistle of a steam engine, and —
for I am bound to confess all to you, Jacintha — I did watch
with keen relish the havoc it was committing. Ere the third
lash fell, the whole surface wore a firey red, which gradually

deepened into violet. Miss De Vere's courage equalled her
strength; she struggled fiercely as ever, and as yet only a mut-
tered execration escaped her. After some thirty such stripes
as she only could give, had exhausted her strength, Martinet
dropped the stump of the third rod, passed a scented handkerchief over her face and neck, and gloated on the mangled spectacle before her.

And now came the strangest of all that day's strange proceedings.

When Martinet had recovered her wind, Renardeau, withdrawing it from somewhere beneath her dress, presented her
principal with a weapon in ludicrous contrast with its gigantic
predecessors. This consisted of a tiny switch, only a few inches
in length, formed apparently of twisted wire. With this between her finger and thumb, Martinet took her stand by the
bedside about half way up, and stooping over the broad end,
looked expressively at us. Helen from experience, I by intui-
tion, guessing her design, sprang wide apart, bearing each a leg
with her, when Martinet by a dexterous turn of her wrist, applied the minute lash between them.

The blow, though a light one, was followed by a cry so wild
and startling, my o'erwrought senses could stand no more. I
was borne, how, or by whom, I know not, to my own room, and
laid upon my bed, where, after swallowing a cordial, I sank at
once into a dreamless slumber.

CHAPTER X.

AFTER THE BATTLE — NOTES COMPARED — A ROD IN PICKLE
FOR MABEL — POSTSCRIPT.

WHEN I awoke, or recovered consciousness, for it was pretty
much the same thing, I was speedily reminded of the late transaction by the pain in my rear. Whenever I stirred there was
a sensation as though crusts were breaking and threads slipping
into the raw flesh. My drawers and petticoats, lying on the

coverlit, reminded me of the inexpediency of putting on any
such garments for the present. What a pickle I must be in!
I arose with difficulty, stood the cheval glass opposite the window, and drew up before it.

The chief damage was in front, for the rods had laced completely round the right thigh, where my unaided eye could trace
the course of the circling birch, every minute knob of which was
"fossil'd," as it were, upon the still blushing skin in that most
tender neighborhood. I then looked over my shoulder into the
mirror and saw : —

Bad as it was, thought I, it is over now, and save a little pain
and stiffness, I none the worse. And, O dear, how hungry I
am! I could swallow even a leg of mutton.

As if in answer to my wants, a savory whiff pervaded my
nostrils, and steps were heard along the passage. I had barely
time to let down, and throw on a loose wrapper, when Helen
entered, followed by Jackson, the latter bearing on a damask
covered tray roast partridges and bread sauce, cripsed potatoes
and butter, jam-tort and trifle, iced water, claret and champagne,
French rolls, Scotch scrones, and grapes in clustering profusion.

Helen had come to sup with me by permission of Martinet,
who had given her carte blanche as to the materials of our
banquet.

Great, doubtless, are intellectual delights; but for pleasure
ever recurring and unalloyed, commend me to the palate.*

When the tray was removed, Helen lighted the candles and
locked the door, and we lay down on opposite lounges for a
cozy chat. I reclined on my left side, facing her; she for reasons good, preferred reposing on her back; her knees were
drawn up higher than her head, her right hand invisible.

"E ben 'tite," she commenced in our school-room French,
"comment la trouves-tu cette Criaillerie?"

---

* Remember that the writer of the above is Miss Doveton. The
reader will have remarked that she is of a sensuous temperament,
dreading pain, and revelling in soft beds and dainty morsels. — *Note
by the Expert.*

"Ah! quel souvenir!"

"I guess," she continued, "what you were doing at the glass. We'll compare notes to-morrow. Mais en effet, what *did* you think of it?"

"O Helen, it was dreadful!"

"Dreadful at first it always is; but was it so throughout?"

"No, I can't explain; there was a change, and it was certainly ecstasy at last. How can that be?"

Helen then offered the same hints about magnetism which I gave you in the beginning of my letter. She asked me when the change took place.

"Directly after I was pulled down again."

"Exactly so — when you were struggling to rise you had one knee up, the other down, and Martinet seized the moment to give the up cut. The rod was so large probably only a single twig got in. One will do, or even a smart cut in the immediate neighborhood. Martinet won't give these cuts to all; there's a lot of the girls, Scatterbrains is one of them, she prefers whipping against their wills, unless she foresees any danger of their making a row about it out of school; then she whips *in* and enslaves them."

"But why does she select some more than others?"

"I can't say; fancy, I suppose. I was the first girl she whipped in this house. It was long ago, when I was not half the size I am now; so she mounted me on her lap and gave it me the very first cut, forcing my legs open. Ever since, though I don't love, I admire her so that I am always ready to take my own share for the privilege of seeing her noble style of birching. How much of her own passions she imparted to you, you best know; but few get it so tight home as the Hon. Miss De Vere, ward in Chancery. Eh! the dour deil! gin I had the taws till her. And Martinet would have let me, too, had we been alone. At least I think so — for once when Dickson, (you know the love she bears me,) told lies in hopes to get me whipped, Martinet walked the pair of us up to the locked room, with never a fourth to help, nor any need of same. Her Majesty with her own royal hands stripped Miss Telltale clean as a whistle to the knees, strapped her tight on to the wooden horse, and handing me a brace of Number Sixes, bade me 'serve her.' Wow, woman, I trow I cuitled her fat tail — T'ould Screechery ne'er hard sic skirlin! And was n't Martinet well pleased? That's how I came by the cairngorm in the brilliant setting."

"O Helen, it seems cruel, but what would I not give to be allowed to do the like! What a favorite you must be with Martinet.

"And so will you be too, Dora, depend on it. Not that she'll trust you with the rod just yet; you must pay your footing first. That glorious what-'ye-ca'-it of your's will procure you the honor of frequent interviews with her Majesty in the Screechery. An't you afraid of the effects of your charms?"

"No — to see and feel what I did to-day *after* the change, I think I could stand it once a week — almost."

"That's brave. Weel, ma beauty, an that be sae, I've blythe speerins. Hearken here, there's to be another whipping tomorrow, one only, but A 1. And what is more, you are a favorite already. You and I are excused school for the day, and are to strip and hold; and a full strip it will be, for she's a stunner, and there will be none present but our four selves."

"O gur-roo, how jolly!" I jumped up and clapped my hands. "Which of the girls is it, Helen?" I asked, going down upon my knees and kissing her as she lay upon the sofa.

"You pretty thing," she said, returning the caress, "stay as you are, and let us have a look at Boppy. Kneel up a bit. Oh! what a wicked Martinet! As Mabel would say : —

'Foul deeds will rise,
Tho' bedgowns cover them to scare men's eyes.'

"Men's eyes! Fancy there was a man there, why, he'd see — Ah! I must not touch it from behind. In front, then? Will that do?"

"Yes, that's nice. Go on and tell me which of the girls it is."

"It's not one of the girls, school-girls, I mean. Have you quite forgotten Mabel?"

"Mabel ! but she 's a servant."

"Only in name. Was ever servant so pretty ? And then for wit and grace few are fit to hold a candle to her. I knew Martinet was dying to be at her, but too proud to make the first advances; so I sounded Mabel, you remember, this morning. My dear, she 'd give her eyes to see the locked room, foreby it 's a recognition and an honor for her to be admitted there. So I brought an humble petition that her Majesty would be graciously pleased to scourge her ever so hard, and let her stay. Martinet likes to keep people in her condition in suspense, and would not let me give her an answer. But to-morrow at twelve, she 'll send for her to her own room, and read her *such* a lecture before she walks her up to the Screechery. Martinet thinks no more of the crime than you or I do, and Sainte Nitouche still less, though she 'll look grave enough to-morrow, I 've no doubt. I hope I shan't laugh in their faces."

"Poor Mabel, what a fright she 'll be in; how I pity her ! "

"Now I don't pity her one whit more than is agreeable and pleasant to my feelings. If she were not frightened at first, there would not be half the fun in seeing her catch it. O Dozy ! of all the whippings I ever was at, your's was the most coco. You could n't faint, no one can that sniffs at Renardeau's bottle ; but you went from white to red and back, your teeth chattering like castanets, and you clung to your clothes as if they were dragging the skin off you. Mabel won't be in half the stew, and would show us all she has for two-pence. Besides, if Martinet 's in a good humor, which she's sure to be with such a beauty, she 'll give her the 'love cut' soon, and after *that* the harder she whips the better pleased Nitouche will be. You should have seen De Vere to-day after she got it."

"Why, what did she do ? "

"What you were going to do, I fancy, when I caught you flying like Vortigern's 'painted Pict.' But you shall hear. After Armstrong had carried you out, Steinkopf and I held her legs ; her Majesty gave her two flicks more in the same place, and then bade them cut her loose. We were all up to the flick trick except Scatterbrains, who screamed, and tumbled head over heels, expecting to be torn to pieces.

"No such thing. La Fonetteuse, as Foxy calls her, flung herself at her Majesty's feet, kissed her hand, pressed it to her breast, and I declare to you she implored her pardon with tears, calling her Mistress — like a little child, and promising thenceforth to do only Martinet's will and pleasure.

"Oh! it was grand. De Vere grovelling on the floor, and to see the way the other drew herself up and said: She hoped the lesson might be of service, but she must have proof of amended conduct before she admitted her on the same footing with the other young ladies. She then ordered us to clear out, and Foxy (that's Renardeau, ye ken), gave the key of the Screechery to Steinkopf, and went off, as she always does, with her Majesty by the private door leading to her bedroom, where it's my belief they —

"Hallo! Ten o'clock. Put out the lights your side, and let's turn in at once, and dream of to-morrow's fun."

POSTSCRIPT

[CRAMMED UNDER THE SEAL.]

Fun indeed it was. Nevertheless, dear Jacintha, even a ship's letter has its limits, and you must fancy the Finale. For when Martinet dismissed us from the Screechery, after whipping Mabel, to whom she gave the "love cut" in style, we three retired to Nitouche's bedroom in a state bordering on frenzy. Had a living man fallen amongst us, we should have torn him piece-meal, like the Bacchantés. As it was, we improvised a man, and ——— Mais, il y a de péchés qui se font sans en parler, et qui paraissent être le résultat d'une folie involontaire.

Some day, perhaps, you may hear of them de vive voix from Your loving Coz.,   DORA DOVETON.

END OF SHREWSBURY HOUSE.

PEN PICTURES.

No. V.

"UP, MISS ALICE, MARCH!"

THE SILHOUETTE.

A PORTION of the canvas, a fourth part,
  Is ruled off for conjecture dim and dread,
A veil diaphanous is drawn athwart,
  Thro' which are guess'd the horrors overhead.
The icy garret and the broken pane,
  The girl groaning in her agony,
The licks and kicks are faintly traced again,
  As on the retina of Alice's eye.
Mama, inclined extremely to one side,
  Is laying into a round shadowy stern,
Two stooping forms *Jane's* prostrate body hide,
  Georgy, erect, is waiting for her turn.
She stands in front, pants down, shift up, and yet,
  Tho' most conspicuous her bottom's swell,
'T is not so shocking, seen *en silhouette*,
  For what the shadow covers none can tell.

SILHOUETTE:

THE PICTURE.

Within, appear snug room and cosy fire,
   View through the window of the wintry snow,
Alice, escaping from the scene of ire,
   Clings to her grandmother, and sobs below.
While whispering comfort, the old lady's eye
Encounters that will give her words the lie.

Enter Miss Kyle beshawl'd, with red-tipp'd snout,
   Her fatal embassy is quickly told:—
"Beg pardon, ma'am. Miss Alice, turn out,
   Your mother waits, don't keep us in the cold."
The voice seems blasted from a big bassoon,
The culprit groans, and falls into a swoon.

The present vanishes, the vision veers
   To rebel roasted writhing on a pike,
To subterranean fires that burn for years,
   To Wolver's wilds, and what Miss Horseman's like;
The dreadful discipline of that old day,
The block brought in, and—"Rouse yourself, I say!"

She wakens slowly to a sense of chill,
   A want of something sheltering below;
There they are lying on the window-sill.
   Ma will be angry if she sees them so.
Angry—Alack! what sounds salutes her ear!
"Come and be whipped,—Cordelia, come here!"

GRANDMAMA'S STORY.

A Ricordamento of the "Good Old Times."

INTRODUCTION.

["An old gentleman " —— We know not what impression these words may convey to the reader's mind; to us they smack either of crabbed dogmatism or senile fatuity. But — "an old lady" should be brisk, chatty, and full of reminiscences of other days. Undoubtedly, the fairer sex mellows best in ageing. One of these antiquities we knew, how nearly related to ourselves is immaterial; who, after she had passed her eighth decade was *impayable*. Her memory then so failed at dinner-time she could not remember the number of glasses of wine she had had, the account of which the old butler, though cautioned, was equally careless in keeping. After she had dozed off this, she would wake like a giant refreshed, to delight us on tête-à-tête evenings with quaint old scandals of the early Georgian period. We, having then attained the, to us, mature age of fifteen, were looked upon by her as a mere infant, certes she treated us with but scant ceremony. In our presence she made no scruple of removing her flaxen periwig the more conveniently to scratch her bare poll; and, unless it were in the dog days, would toast her bare back; or, for the matter of that, her front regions, before the fire, in the most primitive and independent fashion.

Perhaps our relative was exceptionally queer: certain hallucinations she cherished her life through. One was, she would not enter her bed from the side, like other Christians, but must needs lift the clothes and creep upwards from the foot. Another, she would never betake herself to rest without previously removing the valance in search of a robber or assassin whom she supposed to be concealed beneath the bed. In vain her friends tried to dissuade her from thus needlessly fatiguing herself. "My dears," she would reply, "one cannot be too cautious ; better take a little trouble at night than waken in the morning with your throat cut." Tout arrive en attendant. One night it so happened that a prospecting pilferer — he was but a mite of a chimney sweep — did actually select that place of concealment. On detecting him, it were hard to say whether terror or triumph most swayed the old lady, as, pointing with trembling forefinger at the discomfited burglar, she bleated forth, — "There you are, you villain ! I've been seeking for you these sixty years, and found you at last."

"What are these people doing ? " she asked of us one night, as she peered from her drawing-room window into the moonlit portico beneath. It was in the reign of the "Charlies," not "Bobbies," when gas was new and scarce. "What are those *naughty* people doing ? " she repeated. Then, as the truth dawned through her dim optics — "run down, my dear, and tell them to go to bed."

She needed small tuition in ovisuction when her faculties *were* aroused.

We shall not quote any of the anecdotes of our old lady, none of them happening to bear upon the subject now in hand. The following, however, from a female repertory, is àpropose, and we hope may prove acceptable to the reader.]

SYNOPSIS.

RAMBLING RECOLLECTIONS OF ENNISCORTHY, PEEL, WOLVERHAMPTON, AND ABOUKIR — A TICKLISH DOUBT ENLIVENED BY THE RECITAL OF WHAT TOOK PLACE SIXTY YEARS AGO — THE PRETTY BLUSH; THE UGLY ONE — HERE'S MAMA!

"DID you hear about Georgy, Gan ? " Georgy, be it observed, does not wear trousers, at least, not of cloth. Georgy, or Georgiana Graham is a sprightly young lady of thirteen, now reclining on the rug at her grandmother's feet, and looking up with a blank expression of face. Jane and Alice are Georgy's sisters, her elders respectively by three and two years. With all of them "Gan" is a favorite, and deservedly so, she being still a child at heart, and much more companionable than her daughter, Mrs. Graham, who is heard of, not seen. Mr. Graham likewise is invisible, and is a fussy fool.

Now, reader, you know as much of the interlocutors as is needful for the purpose of the story. The old lady being a trifle hard of hearing, we begin again.

Jane. "Gan, did you hear the scrape that Georgy's in ?"

Gan. "No, my dear; I thought something was wrong, and my pretty Peachblossom looks scared. What is it ?"

Jane. "Tell her yourself, Georgy."

Georgy. "Wouldn't deprive you of the pleasure. Tell her you."

Jane. "Wait till I put some coals on first — how the wind does howl — now then, we're snug. Georgy, you must know, was awful naughty."

Georgy. "There you go! Whenever anything is wrong, I'm sure to get the blame."

Jane. "Why, you told me yourself you called Papa a stupid old fool."

Georgy. "He was so aggravating about the letter-bag."

Jane. "Well, anyway he complained to Mama. She's driven off to Bryerly to fetch Miss Kyle, and when they come back, which will be in about an hour's time, Georgy is to be whipped."

Gan. "Miss who ?"

Jane. "Miss Kyle, our governess. You know she is on a visit to her sister, the Bryerly one."

Georgy. "I don't care — at least, only for that beast Kyle. She was always egging on Mama to do it, and now it will be nuts and apples to her. Perhaps Gan might ask Mama to let me off."

Gan. "There would not be the least use in my asking her. Your Mama is resolved, and rightly so, to uphold her husband's authority. And indeed, Georgy, I must say, you deserve the whipping you will get."

Georgy (sotto voce.) "He *is* an old fool all the same."

Alice. "I wonder will she do it with a whip; there is n't such a thing as a rod in the house."

Jane. "Did n't I tell you ? No, — well, I met her in the hall with the bread-knife in her hand and a bundle of twiggs under her arm. I asked her what it was for, and she said we 'd know soon. I think she said we 'd all know, which meant, I suppose, that Alice and I should look on for warning. My faith, Georgy, you would n't say, ' I don't care ' if you had seen what I saw. She must have cut down half the birch tree, at least."

Georgy. "Poof! what is it, after all ? A few skelps that will be over in a minute."

Gan. "Ah ! my child, a minute may contain a deal of pleasure or of pain. Mohammedans believe that the angel Gabriel caught up their prophet at night, bore him through seven worlds, making him spend a lifetime in each, and that a pitcher of water the angel had kicked over in his flight was not run out when they came back."

Georgy. "He! he! hem! I hope my suffering won't seem quite so long. Were you ever whipped when you were a child ? "

Gan. "Aye, that I was, and after. I was whipped at school when I was twenty years of age. The rod was more in use then than now ; boys would come home sick from the floggings they got at school, and for one twentieth part of the impertinence, (cheek you call it,) you all of you give to your papa, any young lady in my day would have been severely whipped."

Jane. "Tell us about your first school-whipping, Gan. You did so once, but that was ages ago."

Gan. "Peachblossom would not like it, I 'm afraid."

Georgy. Oh, yes! I should. I 'd like to know all about it since it must be done. It can't be worse than tooth-drawing, and I can stand that. As for Jane's big bundle, that's no odds ; Annie Glover told me it 's the thin sharp rods that always cut the worst. But go on, darling, and tell us what it's like. Begin at the beginning, there's a love ! "

GRANDMAMA'S STORY.

Gan. "Well, it was the summer of seventeen-ninety-eight, or ninety-nine I think it was, the year after the Irish rebellion broke out. We used to wear scarlet tippets that were called then, Enniscorthy capes. Miss Lumsden's stepfather, that married my aunt Barbary, was killed by the savages and roasted on a pike. He was a major in the old —th ; my poor dear husband commanded the regiment in Egypt, and was one of the two that picked up Sir Ralph after he was shot. The other was an artillery man of the name of Somers. By-the-by, did I not meet him somewhere some years since ?"

Jane. "Yes, at Peel Castle in the Isle of Man ; but that has nothing to do with the matter in hand."

Gan. "No more it has. Well, it was in the summer of '99. I had been at the Firs some weeks, and had got to know all the girls, but specially Mary Lumsden : her stepfather was major in the old —— "

Alice. "What was Mary Lumsden like ?"

Gan. "She was my first cousin by the mother's side, and about my age, which was then seventeen, I think. Mary and I came to the Firs in the same week, and were reckoned like each other, and beauties both, chiefly on account of our complexions, which some of you have, and some of you have n't. The Palmers are all blondes, but of Janet's children only Georgy has the true tint. Not but what you 're handsome girls enough, and indeed, my dears, it 's not always an advantage to have a thin skin. My god-mother, Lady Grandison, used to say she was afraid to touch me. She called mine, sangre azul, blue blood, because I was so proud of my descent from the De la Tremouilles. You know, dear, that I was Charlotte De la Tremouille before I married your grandpapa. Lady Grand ——."

Alice. "What sort of a place was the Firs ?"

Gan. "Much what you would expect from the name. A rambling old pile it was, looking into a common from a scrubby hill covered with larch and firs. Wolverhampton, the nearest town, was some miles off, and all the country round was black and charred. For at Bilston, long ago, a coal-pit having been set on fire by accident or design, and it continued to burn under ground for fifty years."

Alice. "Fifty years — O Gan."

Gan. "Ah! and more than that; Doctor Towers that was rector in my time, made a poem about it. I don't remember how it begun, but it had these lines: —

> That spectre well might horrid thoughts inspire
> By clanking metal and supernal fire,
> Without the hand that lit its nether bones
> To *half-a-century* of reptile groans.

Dr. Towers was a clever man and good scholar. Did I ever tell you how he got his bishopric? He was riding one day — "

Georgy. "O bother Dr. Towers and the king! We know all that bosh."

Alice. "Fie! Georgy, you ought not to speak thus to darling Gan."

Gan. "No, and she ought not to — my sight ain't very good — but —"

Georgy. "Let a be, Gan dear, it 's a pretty 'ittle Puss, it 's going to be vipt, and it 's nice and warm now."

Jane. "For my part, I think about the nastiest thing will be the cold, it 's freezing fast. Fancy having to strip in the attic where she 's sure to do it, with no fire, and the wind whistling through the broken pane."

Alice. "Ugh! and that Kyle with the cross face and purple nose. For all her wraps and rumbelows the critter always seems to be a-cold."

Georgy. "Why do you think Mama will do it in the attic?"

Jane. "The shouting can't be heard through the cross doors. She whipped me once on the old sofa there, and now perhaps — who knows?"

Alice. "Patience, Jane! don't tell me you think that she 'll whip *us.* Speak quick and say you don't."

Jane. "Looks like it, I'm afraid; the bundle was really too big for one."

Alice. "Oh, me! I shall faint at the first stroke. I never could bear pain."

Georgy. "I've been thinking about it, Alice, and *I'll lay my life* she will. Don't you remember how she spoke to you and Jane as well as me, and threatened what she'd do to *all* the next time we were saucy to Papa?"

Jane. "And have n't *we* been civil to him ever since? — except the once — Besides, bah! Alice and I are too big now."

Alice. "Why do you look so, Gan?"

Jane. "Whe—w! I think Gan knows."

Gan. "To tell you a secret, girls, Mama consulted me about that very point the day — and remember it was *after* she had warned you — that you were all so pert to Papa during the ride."

Omnes. "And what did you say?"

Gan. "I put her off, for she was going to have whipped you all three then, and would have done it too, if Kyle had been at hand."

Jane. "But did you not tell her we were much too old?"

Gan. "No, I could not go against my conscience. I told her what I told you, that for such disrespect to parents any girl in my day would have got it well."

Jane. "So then, if we are whipped, we'll have to thank you for it. Je vous en fais mes compliments, madame. Is that curtesy low enough?"

Gan. "It's mighty fine. But indeed, girls, it does make my blood boil to hear the way you speak to your papa, and to your mother too. I could smack you myself at times."

Jane. "You dear old dragon, would it were only you! Go on with your story, please."

Gan. "Alice don't seem too well."

Alice. "Oh! I'm all right — I'm only thinking of the dreadful cold."

Georgy. "The cold is your best friend — Annie Glover says, when Rothwell's girls have notice they'll be whipped, they sit on the bare hearth for hours before."

Alice. "Did Annie ever try the plan herself?"

Georgy. "She did. One time she got a dose for telling lies. Miss Rothwell made her mount on the maid's back, and all the school was wondering at her pluck, while she scarce felt the rods."

Alice. "How so? Had she been sitting on the hearth?"

Georgy. "Better than that. It was in winter time, and she was locked up in the dairy, where she'd been sitting in the butter crocks; when one got warm, she popped into the next."

Alice. "I really think I'll try it. May I, Gan?"

Gan. "May you do what, my dear?"

Alice. "Let down my things and sit upon the hearth."

Georgy. "Hut, child! the hearth won't do with such a fire. Stand on the window stool and clap it to the glass."

Alice. "What if the gardener should pass by?"

Georgy. "Not in the snow; keep your eye on the avenue. That's it, kick 'em right off. Over the shoulders now, and lift the front as well, it's no good while you leave the vitals warm."

Gan. "I'm near-sighted, you know." (But the old lady blushes and turns her head aside.)

Jane. "Well, *'pon my word* that's cool. Why, Georgy, don't you try your own receipt?"

Georgy. "I'm not afraid, but you are looking queer, you'd better ice."

Jane. "No, thank you, I'm not *queer* enough for that. I'll take my chance. Do, Granny, finish the story before she comes."

Gan. "A la bonne heure, si ça vous fait plaisir."

THE STORY RESUMED.

Gan. "The Firs was kept by three maiden ladies, sisters, of the name of Horseman; their mother had kept it before them, and when I went there they had been schoolmistresses themselves for twenty years. The eldest, a big red-faced woman, was the manager; she did the discipline, and her arm was as thick round as Georgy's waist. The others resembled her on a smaller scale, and were quite as bad when they got the chance. Terrible tartars they were all three, and if Mary and I had had a grain of sense, we would have kept clear of their claws; but we were spoilt by flattery, and thought, like Jane and Alice, that we were too big for the rod."

Jane. "Tell the truth, Gan, did Mama say she would whip us all to-day?"

Gan. "No, my dear, she did not. Your Mama is not very communicative, but from what she said on the last occasion, I have little doubt she will."

Georgy. "Oh! you're in for it safe enough. Are we never to get at the bottom of Gan's tale?"

Gan. "The bottom — well, we're coming to that soon. Mary Lumsden was to be punished for something I knew and could prove she had not done. Miss Horseman would listen to no explanation, being tipsy at the time, as indeed she often was. She gave Mary four hours' lock-up for the fault she did not commit, and me the same for taking her part too warmly. When let out we were half mad with rage, and resolved on doing a very wicked thing for which we deserved all the punishment we got and more."

Georgy. "Lor! Gan, I'm glad you had the pluck. What *did* you do?"

Gan. "We stole up at twilight to Miss Horseman's room, and cut to pieces some costly lace and other things, twenty guineas worth at least, we found in one of her drawers."

Georgy. "Hoorah! Serve her right. How did she find you out?"

Gan. (*sneezes*) "Wait a bit — a-psheugh!"

Jane. "Her blood's up now, she'll go on slick."

GAN'S STORY — IN EARNEST.

"We thought no one had seen us, but the following morning on assembling in the school-room we perceived a startling change.

The tables were piled together and Miss Horseman's desk
shifted to the lower end, where the benches were ranged in rows;
over these we spread promiscuously, save that the elder girls generally occupied front seats. Whatever we might surmise, Mary
and I did not know the meaning of this; but the others did, and
looked accordingly, some sad or frightened, the more part
pleased; for a 'block' as it was called, besides gratifying the
bolder spirits that looked on, mostly involved some relaxation
of the day's tasks.

"When the names were called Miss Horseman stepped into
her place; the other sisters stood before the forms, their faces
turned to the desk, and rubbing their fat palms.

"Premising that she should call the attention of all present to
an act of unparalleled malignity, Miss Horseman described in
glowing terms the destruction of her wardrobe; adding that
providentially she had full proof of who the guilty parties were,
of which matter the young ladies themselves should judge. She
then rang a handbell which stood before her on the desk. The
summons was promptly answered by the housekeeper, a sharp-
nosed, ferret-eyed woman, whose glance in passing threw me
into a cold sweat. Being desired by her mistress to state what
she knew of the matter, Wilson deponed thus:—

" 'I was standing, mem, at my storeroom door the last thing,
a going to shet up, when I see two of our young ladies descending down the private stair, that they didn't ought to be, where-
by I noticed their shapes and dress.'

" 'Can you point them out amongst those present?'

" 'Yes, mem, I can; not by name, which I don't but by tokens
as I knows. Them's they, them two waxy ones in laylock slips,
a setting opposite my hand.'

" 'Could you swear to their persons?'

"No, Wilson was not free to swear; it was dusk, and she had
only seen our backs. I held my peace, but Mary boldly repelled
the charge on both our counts.

" 'Vich I thought you would deny it, Miss, and only waited
to see if you would tell that fib. Maybe the t'other un didn't

go straight to the stools, where Miss Priscilla as was fetched by
me see her a coming out; maybe, too, what I found in the room
where you done the devilment isn't one o' yourn. Hah! ye bad
girls, I trust the Missis will cut ye up as ye cut up her things —
sich lace never was for fineness.

" ' See here ! '

"And with a flourish Wilson drew from her pocket a handkerchief marked M. L., which was handed round, compared with
the one she then wore, and recognised as Mary's property. Miss
Horseman asked if the charge was proved, and of course all said
it was. Then her bushy brows were knitted, her eyes flashed,
and her fat throat rolled. Often afterwards I heard that voice
in my dreams, and can remember every word.

" ' Get up,' she said, ' and stand before the desk, that all may
see your shame. Your parents must make good, as far as money
can, the damage done, for which, if I chose, I might send you
both to jail. A heavy balance rests. If I had any doubt or
scruple as to the manner of your punishment, I can have none
now. With liars there is but one way to deal. Go, Wilson,
bid the maids bring in the block, and fetch down four of the
long rods.'

"A voice behind said — ' That's two a piece, and long ones.
Won't they yell.' "

Omnes. "Why do you stop ? "

Gan. (smiling) "To give them time to come —

                                        "In the interim,
though my teeth chattered and my tongue would scarcely move,
I ventured to plead that I had never said I was not there.

" ' You paltry coward,' she replied, ' you would have screened
yourself with your companion's lie. I shall punish you as
severely as I shall her. Resume your place.'

"During this colloquy Wilson had returned unseen by me,
and had laid her burden somewhere out of sight. She now
stood at the half-open door ; when she flung it wide two maids
entered bearing a sort of wooden couch with stool attached, such
as was used in most of the great schools. This they set down

when told, and stood one at each side of it, in sleeveless bodies and skirts of serge, for servants were servants then, and dressed for work not show. These two were strapping wenches chosen for their strength in case a big girl should refuse the rod. They smiled furtively, whispered each other, and then looked at me. About Mary's condition there could be no doubt, she being already seized. Miss Grace and Miss Priscilla, whose business it was to strip, walked her between them to the upper end where the block was, and commenced the work with savage zeal. Wilson stood by with pincushion in hand."

Jane. "Was there much stripping?"

Gan. "I might say yes or no to that. Buckram and farthingale were out, and in revenge the rising generation looked like dolls, and scarce wore anything but shift and gown. Stays there were none, the waist served up the breasts as on a dish, and clasped behind between the shoulder-blades, the skirts adhering to the shape below. This led to shocking scenes in girl's schools, where, as I said before, it was customary to whip those of quite a marriageable age. To insure a thorough strip little more was needed than to take down the web drawers, which hooked in front and came up breast high to keep the vitals warm. This was seldom done without more or less resistance, and when done the skirts were furled to the armpits front and rear, and fastened round the throat. The nudity of the bath would have been decent compared to these fights and the sexual exposure they involved."

Jane. "But if the strippers stood in front, they must have hid the view."

Gan. "Not during the twists; besides I have not done; when you know all, you will understand how impossible it was to hide what ought not to be seen. There were two junior teachers there, poor young women apprenticed to Miss H., who made no scruple to flog them before us all. After their heads were hid, we could tell which was which by only looking at them from behind."

Jane. "La, what a shame ! Mama will soon be back; get on with the story, please."

Gan. "Mary was too sensible to fight ; when her things were fixed in the manner I have described, she was handed to the maids, who placed her on her knees upon the stool and gently pushed her body down till her mouth touched the cushioned part. The sisters then returned for me and dragged me up, inclining to one side so as not to intercept the view, the school-girls being ranged in rows behind, some mounted on the forms. When we reached the whipping-place they took off my scarf and sash, but did no more just then, being intent on what was going on.

"Mary had yielded sullenly, and lay motionless upon the block ; deep silence reigned. Miss Horseman left her desk, tramped up the room, and took her station to the left and rear. She drew the glove from her right arm and handed it to Wilson, who advanced with the long rods."

Jane. "Why do you call them long ? Were they birch rods ?"

Gan. "No, my dear, Wolver is not like this shire where birch abounds. With us canes of all sorts and sizes were in use. For trifling faults the culprit got it with a slim rattan on the bare hands and arms ; for graver ones she was held upon a form and beaten on the broadest part with a thick bamboo over the thin clothes. These punishments, though painful, were not reck-oned much of a disgrace, but we were to be treated in a differ-ent fashion. For crimes so flagrant as ours was reserved a weapon of exceptional severity. This consisted of a short stout stick, to which were attached three lithe willow wands, that, when flung, extended some feet in length and gave a triple whiplike cut that lapped around the loins."

Alice. "*Ow-wow.*"

Jane. "Did not you flesh creep ?"

Gan. "My dear, I was so scared I scarce knew whether I stood upon my head or heels. At first I could think only of the pain, but when I looked upon the shocking sight in front — for there it lay before me big and bare — shame sent the blood up to my face and neck. And now I must tell you of a curious thing I never saw before or since, a thing that many won't believe. There were two Miss Cranstons there, co-heiresses, their uncle Sir Neil left them six thousand each, besides Dean Cranston's money, share and share alike. The eldest the year after she left school was married to the Cómte de Houtovolée, son to the Duc de la Vieilleroche ; he was connected with the De la Tremouilles by —— "

Jane. "O Gan, don't mind that now. The curious thing ? "

Gan. "Eh, dear ? Oh, aye ! Miss Cranston, no, Bell it was, had tried to leave the room, the door of which was at the upper end. Being ordered back, she was passing, pale as death, while Mary was in the act of kneeling down. What she then saw made her turn so red that every eye was fixed on her. My cousin's face I could not see, being behind, but at the moment that Bell Cranston blushed, that part of Mary's person that was facing me blushed too."

Georgy. "Her bottom, do yon mean ? Ha !— ha !"

Gan. "Ah ! you may laugh. Often I laughed myself at the story of the Corday blushing when the bourreau slapped her face after the head was off. But here was a whole body and a living heart able to send the current either way. The fact was so ; the part blushed visibly in both the cheeks ere ever it was struck, and then turned pale again. I mentioned this years afterwards to Mrs. Cox that she might tell me what her husband thought. He said the change of color could not be attributed to mental emotion, for that would send the blood up to the head, and that it must have been caused by some slight pressure and the fineness of the skin. You don't remember Dr. Cox — no — Graham was courting Janet at the time that he was carried off by the dreadful jail fever that broke out in —— "

Jane. "But the whippings, Gan ? "

Alice. "Tell us all about them ; were they hard ? "

Georgy. "Did they last long ? "

Gan. "Less than a minute each, about as long as you would be counting forty by a watch; for Miss Horseman, when she did begin, whipped quick, and only stopped to change, giving us twenty strokes a piece, or sixty lashes of the three-tailed rod. Oh! girls, I think I feel it now; it hurt most here."

Jane. "Your cousin was whipped first?"

Gan. "Yes. After a cutting speech addressed to both, Miss Horseman chose a rod, and looking sternly at Miss Grace, pointed to Mary's drawers, for they were tight and clung around the thighs. When this was rectified, up rose the huge bare arm. She did not seem to put forth extra strength, yet the effect was magical. In an instant the whole surface was discolored, not with a rosy blush, but with livid weals and angry blue black red. The weapon whirred, whopped on the flesh, and rose again with the force and precision of a steam hammer."

Jane. "How did she bear it?"

Gan. "Better than I. She had been resting on her arms, her head bent down, as was the rule in this disgraceful punishment. At the first cut she started and cried "Oh!" then grinding her teeth till her cheeks swelled, and her mouth frothed, she knelt bolt upright, favored by the maids, who liked her pluck, for they were used to tears and screeching. When the rods were changed, Miss Horseman ordered them to pull her down. This was not effected without a notable struggle. Once down, even Mary Lumsden was powerless; she tried to rise by straightening her legs and standing on her toes, which did no good, and laid her open to worse treatment. The whipping recommenced with added force, blue beads sprang up and trickled down the thigh, and ere the twentieth stroke, the blood flowed freely."

Jane. "Did she not roar?"

Gan. "She kicked, and bounced, and twisted on the stool; but, stubborn to the last, not even a whimper or a sob escaped her."

Georgy. "Bravo! I vow Mama shan't get a squeak from me."

Jane. "Oh, yes! you 're brave with only a birch rod. How would you like the flail?"

Georgy. "I think the birch will get it out of *you*. We 'll see which stands it best."

Alice (*impatiently.*) "Your turn came next?"

Gan. "Without a moment's pause. Directly Miss Horseman dropped the point, Miss Priscilla caught me by the throat and bent me back against her knee, Wilson pulled up my clothes in front, and Miss Grace attacked my drawers. I screamed and fought them off until the servants had to come in aid, and them, being mad with fright, I kicked upon the shins. To save themselves they tore through hook and eye, and skinned me like a hare. Pulling the shift over my ears, they dragged me to the block; some one rapped my legs with the stick end of the rod, which brought me to my knees; then four horny hands were pressed upon my neck; the fore-part of my body being forced down, the hind——"

Jane. "Hush! Did n't I hear wheels?"

Georgy (*runs to the door and looks through the key-hole.*) "The chaise has just drawn up, they 're coming in, and — as I live, she 's brought the other, too."

Jane. "What other?   Can't you speak?"

Georgy. "Cordelia Kyle; Cordy, her sister calls her. She's twice as big as ours, and——"

Alice. "Oh! oh! Mama is calling us all three."

Jane. "Did she call me by name?'

Georgy. "Aye, that she did; what then? it 's *only* a birch rod. Here, Alice, take my arm."

Grandmama (sola.) "Ah, me! I wish I was in bed. Alice is sure to scream. I hope they 'll close the cross door."

(*Alice bursts in, pale and dishevelled, and flings herself into her Grandmother's arms.*)

Alice. "Oh! Oh! Oh! I could n't stand it, Gan. Let me rest a moment on your kind bosom before I die."

Gan. "Courage, my love, it 's only a common whipping such as girls get. After all, it may not hurt as much as you suppose."

Alice. "Not hurt! on the naked flesh, and with Mama in such a rage! If you had seen her beating Jane."

(Voices heard on the stairs.)

First Voice. "She's in there with the old lady. I hear her sobs."

Second Voice. "Shall I go in too?

First Voice. "No; stop where you are, unless I call you."

Enter Miss (chez elle) Kyle.

Miss K. "Beg pardon, ma'am. Turn out, Miss Alice, and be whipt, both your sisters are done ; shame for *you* to keep us in the cold."

Gan. "I think the child is in a swoon."

Miss K. "Swoon! fid—— Rouse yourself; don't tell me you 're fainting with your foot going like that. I would not use force before you if I could help it, ma'am. Speak to her, please."

Gan. "Alice, it *must* be done, and the sooner the better. Go at once."

Alice. "I *can't*, Boo-hoo! the pain will kill me; I shall die of fright."

Miss K. "It's no use talking. *Cordelia, come here!*"

PEN PICTURES.

No. VI.

LE PEDAGOGUE MALGRE LUI.

WHY should the pedagogue act *malgré lui?*
  You, my good sir, it may be safely said,
Were never bidden by a matron free
  To hold beneath the rods a bouncing maid,
Too big and bold for birching on the knee.
  If so, your virtue halted, we're afraid.
"Whipping grown girls" is a pastime rare
  Few males, if called on, *could* refuse to share.

The woman wooes the warrior to his fall,
  The payer orders it, the paid obeys;
The "pedagogue per force" has got a haul
  That Flora Foljambe's figure half displays;
Her head enveloped in the Paisley shawl,
  He holding her mauve dress above the stays;
One heavy hand keeps down the smother'd end,
  The other, bashful, hovers o'er the bend.

Naughty no doubt, but she's a child, you know,
  Her pants being up you can't dispute it, mind;
Her mother says she is, if you say no,
  Look where the fire lights it from behind;
Haply examined by the ruddy glow,
  Some proof without hair-splitting you may find:
Again you're baffled, for, so close the fit
  Nothing escapes, if there — probatum sit.

De Lancey fain the promised land would spy.
  His fingers, itching to undo the back,
Know not the trick, nor does he dare to try
  Lest *she* mean otherwise.   But here comes Mack!
Pride in her port, and passion in her eye,
  Ready to kiss, perhaps — resolved to smack.
The mountain birch depends in graceful showers,
  She 'll do no treason to its stinging powers.

WANTED, AN HEIR.

A Tale in Two Chapters.

CHAPTER I.

THE HEIR "SANS" LOI — FROM CONSTANTINOPLE TO CANTIRE — THE DREAM-PIPE.

IN France, remarked an illogical writer, there is no primo-
geniture. Yet in France the loi salique obtains upon the throne,
and in England everywhere else. Unless by special enactment
the British female, as such, cannot succeed to landed property;
failing male heir, ancestral halls, woods, lakes, and mountains,
pass to other hands.

> " The place that knew them,
>   Knows them now no more."

To wrest an inheritance from its rightful line murder has
been done, and when detected all men execrate the deed. But
to create is blessed: "increase and multiply," saith holy writ.
When godliness is gain, it cannot be matter of surprise should
husbands sometimes wink, and wives be guilty of a pious fraud.
Dire was the predicament of Roderick Roy Macdonald, lord of
Glencabra and of half Cantire. In his line had run for centuries the headship of a powerful clan; he owned thousands of
acres on the mainland, with feudal rights extending over numerous isles, on one of which he had a princely home. All these
pleasant things, failing male heir, threatened to pass to a kins-
man whom his soul abhorred.

In early youth, Macdonald had married for love a beautiful

but consumptive girl, who, after ten years barren union, passed away, and now the chief resolved to marry for an heir. With this end in view, he selected the charming Widow Foljambe, née Meggy Macdonald of the clan. Her first husband perished by an accident ere the wedding night, yet had she given proof of fecundity by the production, in due time, of a thumping babe, a female, it was true — but such a one!

Descriptions are sad bores; do what you will, they all seem stereotyped, and to purloin even the worst is felony in bookcraft. Here, to save trouble, we will venture on a crib from the engraver's steel. Let the reader recall the illustrated edition of the "Widow Married"; let him conjure up the ci-devant Barnaby, voluptuous, ringleted, and rosy-cheeked, watching the bouncing Patty O'Dona*gough* (cré nom! — who ever heard the like?) as she plays at ship billiards with her lovely Jack. Let him do that, and he will have the personal appearance of our heroines; their characters will unfold themselves further on.

At the period of the present tale, our ex-widow, apparently verging on the three *fs*, owned reluctantly to thirty years, while Miss, a reputed twelve year old, on the warrant of a locked-up Bible, claimed to be sixteen. Child or not, the charms of Flora Foljambe threatened already to eclipse those of her Mama, whose vanity and love of power were great; hence it came that little love was lost between the pair.

More years went by, and still the second union was unblessed. The fault clearly lay with the chief himself, who by youthful excesses had impaired a vigorous constitution. He was now at Malvern, seeking to restore the tension of his nerves through the instrumentality of the water-cure. When that translucent humbug first oozed out, it was thus referred to by a critic in the Quarterly Review : —

"We were watching the flirtations of a sick duck with the pond in our yard: first he paddled ankle-deep, contented with a fuss-bad; next venturing further in, he treated himself to a leib-bad; finally he took the prescribed Kopf-bad thus: — elevating his rump, he depressed his head, reversed the process

and opened wide his bill. We thought he was going to shout
—Hurrah for Vincent Priesnitz ! All he said was — ' Quack !
quack ! quack ! "

Shift we the Kaleidoscope.

It is ten o'clock on a November morning in London, foggy
of course. The back recesses of the coffee-room in the Craven
Hotel, Strand, have a gas-jet flaming over succulent hams and
joints. The majority of the visitors, however busy may be their
jaws in mastication, preserve an unbroken silence, taking their
pleasure, if such it be, molte tristement, as old Froissart says.
About all, save one, there is an unmistakably London air. But
in that more open box on the right of the front fireplace, sits a
youth of singular prepossessing appearance, to whom all seems
new and bright. This is Captain Sir Thomas De Lancey, just
landed from a Balaclava transport, after being slightly wounded
at the Redan. In the long interregnum between the Peninsular
and Crimean wars, your Captain was an article of tardy growth,
often grizzled and discontented. De Lancey, when he obtained
promotion and the Victoria Cross for gallant deeds, scarcely
numbered more than twenty years ; yet, though but slight down
shaded his upper lip, his bronzed complexion and erect bearing
showed him no carpet night.

During his absence on service, De Lancey's father died, and
his family emigrated to Australia, a savage land too far for him
to reach. Having six months' leave and a tolerable credit in
Craig's Court, our Captain resolved to enjoy himself in Europe,
heading from London in such direction as chance or inclination
might prompt. The metropolis itself, in the absence of all acquaintance, possessed for him few attractions, and revolted him
by its sordid greed of gain. De Lancey had used the Craven in
his schoolboy days, and was green enough to expect a personal
recognition on his return from the wars. In that Caravanserai,
guests were known only as "No. So-and-so," the "two brandies
and water," or haply, when Crimean heroes thickened, as "the
gent with the harm hoff." Yet there was apparently the same
staff as in former days, the perennial boy in buttons, the solemn

waiter gliding about in listed slippers, limp white choker, and baggy black cloth. De Lancey looked hard at this functionary, a faint souvenir of half-crowns illuminated his flabby features, and for a moment touched the waiter's soul, and thus he spoke:—

"Capital 'am, sir, fust cut. Prefer somethin 'ot? Rasher and heggs in three minutes. Post, 'Tiser, Times."

Hollow was that waiter's friendship; the proffered sheet of "Times" contained no word of news; its forty-eight columns was filled with As-*es*, Wanted-*s* and Lost-*s*. Amongst the advertisements, the first that caught De Lancey's eye, was the following, in French:— "On demande une cuisinière *brogue*, de religion Catholique, pour une famille aristocratique, qui lui garanterait de gages satisfaisants. On expliquera les motifs qui font désirer la perte d' un œil à la personne qui se présentera." *

Strange, thought the Captain; in Greek they call a one-eyed monster *Cook*-lops. Can that have anything to do with it? By a freak of diva Fortuna, a name he knew at length arrested his gaze. The advertisement in which it appeared, ran thus:—

WESTERN ISLES. — A lady, unable to procure masters on the spot, wishes to hear of a gentleman competent to assist in the education of her daughter. He must be a good modern linguist, and produce undeniable references. Board and liberal salary for six months. Application to Messrs. Scarlet and Tapes, Solicitors, Chancery Lane.

Odd, again, mused the Captain, six months, just my time. "Must be a good linguist." Gad — If French, German, Italian, and a smattering of Dutch will do, I'm her man. Wonder who the lady is — Scarlet and Tapes, family solicitors ——."

"Boy, bring me my boots."

In half an hour he had threaded the eye of Temple-bar, turned leftward down the tortuous precincts of the law, and was

* This actually appeared in the "Times," about November, 1865.

swallowed up in the cave of the mythical Scarlet and too real Tapes. The last-named gentleman sat, as of yore, bolt upright in an atmosphere of *deeds*, not words. He received his military client with some show of courtesy, and even vouchsafed a curt inquiry or two on general topics, till warned by the wandering of his parboiled eye, De Lancey opened the matter in hand.

"This advertisement," producing the paper. "What does it mean ? "

"Scotch lady — languages — wants daughter taught."

"Would I do ? "

Tapes pushed up his glasses to obtain a clearer view, then answered with a grim smile — "Yes."

"How can you tell my qualifications for the task ? "

"Know any foreign tongue ? "

"I was educated abroad, and can speak three fluently."

"You'll do."

"But why ? "

"My dear Sir," (for an instant he ceased to be eliptical,) *"my dear Sir!* professional. Instructions recommend gentleman, young and — so forth. Snug berth, hundred pounds —— "

"Own name ? "

"Does the lady know it ? "

"No."

"Then without titles. Yes."

A few strokes of the pen furnished the credentials, and the route was imparted in still fewer words. Two days more saw our hero located in the lower Western Isles, which locality if the reader would have described, let him, or her, order a pictorial tour to Cantire, by Cuthbert Bede, author of "Verdant Green." If that most pleasant tour clear up no other mystery, it will give at least no end of view of a Scotch lassie's legs.

De Lancey carried in his countenance a better recommendation than the attorney's, while his frank and soldierly bearing procured him welcome "baith in bower and ha." Need we say that his patroness was Mrs. Macdonald, of Glencabra? Mother and daughter vied in attentions to their handsome guest; his only embarrassment lay in the keenness of the competition. It was evident Mama would brook no rival, and till her supremacy was assured, the innocent third party was occasionally both hen and chicken pecked.

We will leave unrecorded the events of the first few days, taking up matters where they tended to a crisis, *cum stridore acuto*, as old Horace says.

It is late; Flora Foljambe has been sent to bed. De Lancey and Mrs. Macdonald are practicing duets on the piano after supper and champaign. Her eyes are unduly bright, her cheeks ablaze. Her dress of amber satin is cut square in front. The direction of beauty is commonly reckoned to be curvilinear; much, however, may be said in favor of the square cut, if truly square; and our grandmothers, from whom the simple fashion was borrowed, and as usual improved, were not wont to err on the score of prudery:—

> "Loose and bonny were they a
> When they pit on their breast knots."

The diaphanous muslin that edged Mrs. Mack's square-cut satin was a patent humbug.

The singers sit close, the air is amorous and sad. At its close they are startled by the apparition behind them of a "woman in white"—and black—bedgown, but no nightcap to restrain the shower of jet.

"Mama, I want the key of the wardrobe, it is on your bunch."

"Gracious, child, what brings you here in such a state?"

"I told you before. I want the wardrobe key."

"What for?"

"Oh, dear me! there's things of mine there."

"Nothing you can possibly require. Be off to bed, and don't plague."

"How busy we are; I'd bolt the door if I were you. Mr. De Lancey seems to like the '*waist of time.*'"

"'I'll punish you for *that*. Go up at once. And, Mr. De Lancey, I should advise your keeping your doors locked, if you would not have your letters read by that ——"

"I did n't ; it 's a lie."

"A what ? "

But Flora had fled, dropping a slipper in her haste ; Mama was after her, their voices heard in wordy contest up the stairs.

The harmony of the evening was destroyed, and as the hall clock tolled twelve, De Lancey put out the lights, and retired to smoke the pipe of contemplation in a fire-lit den.

We say "fire-lit" advisedly, because the heaped fir-logs shed a ruddy glow that would have dimmed the taper's flame. His gun and game-bag hung upon the wall ; a tired pointer snoozing on the rug greeted his entrance with a lazy wag. A kettle simmered on the hob ; the table offered all appliances for drink ; the square armed chair was bolstered like a bed ; a tall chibouk, already primed, stood by the fire-side.

Et voilà pourquoi nous l'avous nommée "la Pipe aux Rêves."

Because that pipe held more than Latakia. Within its bowl his hostess was enshrined, waiting the rousing spark to float forth in fume, followed by kindred forms, like genii in Eastern tales. That night, ere Flora interposed (plague on the jealous jade!) he had reason good to think of Mrs. Mac with *hope* — more than a thousand proofs of her good will. What the convincing token was the pedal might have seen, if it had eyes. Had Flora seen ? Then Flora floated on the fragrant cloud. How impudent the handsome hussy was ! Her legs were bare ; she could have had only shift and bedgown on, yet such a swell behind ! A whipping certainly would do her good. He heard the threat distinctly on the stairs, not general, but particular : — "I 'll whip your — something — Miss," Mama had said, intoning the last word. How could it be ? Flo. was too big for birching on the lap, and much too bold. But there were other modes, and aid at hand — aye, even overpowering odds. Were there not the two huge housemaids, Kate and Jean ? Macdonalds both, sib, if not sisters, to the laird.

Up rose these nymphs, all in athletic buff, even as his eyes had seen them in the flesh last Sabbath morn.

An early riser, De Lancey had then surprised the pair at their ablutions in the scullery. That day was honored by a special scrub, and there they were, as Tony says, — "in a concatenation accordingly" — stripped to the hips and slippery with suds. Hech, sirs, the battle royal that issued. They dodged and dived, he caught them where he could; their scanty skirts forsook them in their flight, and then they turned to bay. Lacing their arms behind his back, they forced him through the door, and ere they went within, each clasped him panting to her billowy breasts, and gave the kisses that he could not take.

Now Madam Mack was mistress and more of every vassal there ; even Flora often trembled at her frown, and shrank from the raised hand. He had seen her ears well boxed — presumptive proof of worse behind the scenes. Empty indeed ! After such a shrewd retort, the threat is certain to be carried out, the time is *now*.

The clouds resolve themselves into an upper room where Flora is confined. Mama comes in armed with a scourge ; the giant sisters follow in her wake; she waves her hand, instant the wraps are off, the rebel bare. Flora is high on Kate's capacious back — how broad it was he knew. Jean in reserve watches the chieftainess tanning Flo's toby with terrific taws !

Ho ! by the Prophet's beard, a blest chibouk ! Although his waking senses be debarred, may Allah grant a vision of the night. Ah ! qu'ils nous font plaisir ces charmants rêves humides ! He smacked his lips and mixed a fresh rummer with Glenlivat's dew. That liquor is seductive as innocent. In its praise, as we don't bother him with head-verses (though many a one we know), will the respected reader tolerate a tail ?

"Pherson had a son
  Married Noah's daughter,
Nearly spoilt ta Flood
  Drinkin oop ta water;

"Whilk he wad ha deen,
  (I at least believe it)
Had ta mixture been
  Only pure *Glenleevat*."

BON GUALTIER.

CHAPTER II.

STORM IN A TEA-CUP — THE CONJECTURAL CIGAR — THE REAL THING — THE HEIR FOUND.

ON the following morning De Lancey came in from a five miles walk, glowing with health, and disposed to enjoy the plenteous meal. To two of the trio, however, that breakfast must have been the reverse of satisfactory. The "gunpowder" seemed to impart an explosive quality to the imbibers, and the tongue of the "stall'd ox" had plenty of the proverbial seasoning. In short, the ghost of last night's quarrel was by no means laid, and it was evident that a duel had yet to be fought between the pair. In vain De Lancey tried some pleasant theme; they answered vaguely and with vapid smiles, their eyes the while watching each other's motions with a lynx-like leer, Their veins were swollen and their lips compressed; the cups and saucers rattled in their hands. An explosion had nearly been brought about at last by Miss Flora choosing, whether through accident or by design, to jerk her spoon so as to flirt the tea upon her mother's dress. Old Donald, the deaf butler, then came in to take away, under whose cover she effected a dignified retreat. Mama sprang up with a half-muttered curse, slipped a key into De Lancey's hand, and said with emphasis while passing out—

"Wait till the beds are made, then *look into your top drawer*."

He started, nodded acquiescence, and passed through the conservatory into the garden. There he lighted a cigar, and sought a seat — "as was his custom in the *ante*-noon."

> " Snug in an English garden's shadiest spot
> A structure stands and welcomes many a breeze,
> Lowly and simple as a ploughman's cot,
> There monarchs may unbend who wish for ease.
>
> " There sit philosophers, and sitting read,
> And to some end apply the dullest pages,
> And pity the barbarians north of Tweed,
> Who scout these fabrics of the southern sages."

The barbarians are less barbarous now; for here, be-north
the Tweed, is a temple, neat enough in summer with white-
wash, ivy, and in-peeping rose. In this frosty December morning, indeed, the dry leaves rattle in the corners, and in the
deep groined window lies the hermit spider, wrapped in his
fluffy integument, dreaming perhaps of past or future flies.
We too have our flies, gaily pursued in fancy, and when caught
in fact, do they not all prove to be flies wanting the first letter ?
No, not always. For once, De Lancey, giving the loosest reign
to conjecture, had failed to overtake the magnitude of the boon
which capricious Cupid was about to bestow on him.

On re-entering the hall he heard the mistress calling to the
maids, and peeping through a passage door, beheld the last with
pail and clout descending the back stairs. Up the same he
mounted, three steps at a time, passed from the sitting to the
bedroom, applied the key, and tore open the top drawer.

Reader, suppose in lieu of the advertisement sheet, the waiter
at the Craven Hotel, Craven street, Strand, had supplied our
hero with the morning news — "where'er his wanderings might
have been," that drawer had never been unlocked by him, nor
would he have seen that which now lay bristling under his
shirts, and took away his breath — to wit, —

Six slips of mountain birch fitting in length the drawer, the
branches curling to the sides, the stems compressed into a
souple stick, that wooed the grasp with crossed and waxy cord
to test its spring. A weapon terrible to culprit's flesh, only to
look on which inflicted like the surgeon's knife a prescient pang.
Appended to the handle by a silken thread was a note, dont
voici le contenu.

"TUESDAY, 12 P. M.

" DEAR SIR, — I shall whip Flora to-morrow, (to-day
" rather) for the outrage you witnessed, and for other
" things. I regret to say she has been in the habit of
" opening your desk with the key of hers, which happens
" to fit it. I surprised her lately in the act of reading your
" correspondence, and threatened her with the rod. She

" then showed such a mutinous spirit I saw I could not
" manage her alone. As she must be punished, and on
" your account, I reckon on your aid to hold her for me.
" I shall leave the rod at hand, and look into the lesson-
" room as soon after breakfast as I can. Meanwhile do not
" let her think you know what is to be. She is prepared
" to evade any attempts of mine, assisted by the maids, but
" will not suspect one there. I shall whip her kneeling
" at a chair; directly I point it out, place her in the right
" position, keep her shoulders down, and leave the rest to
" me.

" Faithfully yours,   " M. M."

" P. S. — Only *severe chastisement* will do her any good.
" Remember this when the time comes, and on no account
" let her get up till I have done.
" *Burn this when read.*"

De Lancey read the perfumed poulet twice, to assure himself
of the fact announced, poising the palpable evidence the while.
Although his own rear tingled in his trews, the touch of the
right end filled him with cruel longings to lay on, or better still,
to see it done by *her*. He could not be without natural resent-
ment when he thought of the free remarks of his correspondent,
based partially on his own revelations from head-quarters, sub-
mitted to the scrutiny of a prying minx, who, to obtain the
knowledge, had violated the sanctuary of his desk. It was a
childish act; her mother, who should know best, said she was a
child. If so, a whipping, and a sound one, was her due, and
he being ordered by his employer so to do, was bound to assist.
When the paths of duty and inclination happen to be parallel,
what Catos we can be! Again, he looked at and brandished
the elastic birch, and thought where its twigs were to be applied, and by what arm; an arm the naked symmetry whereof
last night had driven him wild; she, too, had suffered him to
kiss it unrebuked — to do even more — and now invited him to
see her wield the rod!

Vengeance could not be her sole object; for that, horsewhip or cane would have sufficed, but birch would be innocuous on the back. Flora, he knew, wore stays; besides, he was to keep her shoulders down. It must be then the other end — those graceful twigs could hurt only the bare flesh — or nearly so — Ah! that perhaps was it. Even so, to whip at all much clothes must be removed from off a stern that rivalled even Mama's in swell. Still, it was the thought of Mrs. Mack that fired him most. Those eyes, so fierce to all, to him so mild — that sensuous form that loved to press to his. Flora would, doubtless, be dismissed when whipped —

And then !

Between the ticklings of time's clock how many thoughts may crowd! But now "the real thing" is drawing on.

If the gudeman's "vera step had music in't," what thrilling notes sounded from Flora's feet

"As *she* cam up the stair !"

The pédagogue malgré lui had barely time to hide the symbol of his craft and occupy a seat, when his fair pupil entered, omitting all salutation, and leaving wide the door. The morning being keen, she made straight for the fire, stood back to it, and pitched her books on to the table under the magisterial nose. In Flora's breast two passions were at war. She admired De Lancey for his wit and handsome looks, and would have been more tender had he not shown such marked preference for Mama; as it was, this made her manner at all times brusque, and often, as at present, downright rude.

"Pick up," she cried, "there's one of those plagues dropped. I've been trying a new dress, and my fingers are quite numbed. But, gudesake mon, what gars ye glower sae?"

"I was thinking of your misconduct yesterday."

"Eh, didn't she rile me, though, locking up my dress as though I were a child? I got the key at last; no thanks to her. An't it a pretty mauve; how does it sit behind?"

"It don't become you, Miss Foljambe; you put it on without your mother's leave, and stole the key."

"Bow-wow! and if I did, what's that to you? You are here to teach me languages only. Pray, *Mister* De Lancey, if that's your name, what have *you* got to say to my conduct to Mama?"

"More than you think, perhaps. And, indeed, my dear, I would advise you as a friend to treat her with more respect."

"Fiddle-de-dee! I don't respect her one bit, and as for *you*, d'ye think I did n't see? One arm was round her waist, round part of it at least; what you were doing with the other hand, she knows best; her great blowsy face was ―――― "

At this juncture, Mama, having overheard the dialogue outside, stepped in, looking pale and dangerous, and closed the door. Without a word she pushed the table to one side, wheeled forward the arm chair from which De Lancey rose, and placed ominously gaping before the startled Flo, who blenched and shifted uneasily, but seeing no weapon, could not comprehend the move. That done, in thick and hurried utterance, Mrs. Mack announced her will.

"I promised you a whipping, and whipped you shall be, if I have to summon half the house and have you tied. I *will*, you stubborn minx, I'll flog you well. De Lancey, you saw that ― that girl's insolence, help me to punish her, or *go* and send up both the maids."

"I'll aid you, madam, if it must be so. But pray, pray suffer me to intercede. I trust, if Miss Flora makes due submission, you will overlook her fault."

"After the renewed insult? Ha-ha! No-o-o. Catch her, make haste!"

Speechless with rage and shame, Flo. darts across the room. That instant she is pinned by powerful arms, dragged back, and forced face downwards on the chair. In the act of kneeling, Mama whisks up her skirts behind, packs them tight-drawn beneath the captor's hands, lifts and tucks in the pendant front, and moulds the doomed posteriors to a crescent form. She then unclasps her heavy Paisley shawl, wraps it thrice round the

clamorous head, secures it with a knot, and passes to the next
room for the rod.

In vain Flo. writhes and roars to be let go. Her voice sounds
hollow in the triple folds; her arms are pinioned to her sides;
her shoulders levelled by resistless force. One of the tutor's
hands secures the skirts; the other toys around the baffling
breeks, that overlap and do not *break* at all. Will *she* leave on
the screen, he dares not—knows not, indeed, how to—move?
Mama meditates no such treason to the stinging birch. Returning armed, she lays the weapon on the culprit's back, her jewelled fingers dive beneath the stays, the slit panjammies tumble
wide apart, and heaps of flesh appear.

The fire warms them pleasantly enough; full soon they will
be hotter than she likes. Mama has taken her stand a little to
the left, and holds out her right arm; he hands the rod, looking
unutterable things, and blushing blue. One instant she returns
a conscious glance, then following the direction of his eye, she
shakes the birch, and vengeance clouds her brow.

"Stand clear !"

In his zeal De Lancey had craned over the imperilled parts;
warned by the cry, he draws back just in time —

A flash — a crash — a howl !

Ere he can trace the cause, the snow turns crimson 'neath the
rapid rod; the air is shrill with stripes, cut follows cut, and
groan succeeds to groan; and yet, *as yet*, the blushes are un-
spoilt, the longer twigs assault the tenderest parts and leave
their impress there. The limbs launch out in all-revealing
kicks, the muffled head spins frantically round, a pent volcano
rumbles in the cloth ———

Mrs. Mack is beside herself, and looks more like a maniac
than the handsome woman that she *was*. Her hair was broken
loose and flops into her face, she does not stop to bind it. Careless of appearance, since Flora cannot see, she clutches up her
clothes with the left hand as high as though she were preparing
her own person for the rod; the sturdy limbs exposed vouch for

the power to hurt; the will to do so glares in her savage eye. Did not the bared body of her rival afford scope for her jealous fury, she must have vent it on her lover, whose excitement was now scarce less than hers.

But De Lancey, why did he sanction such inhuman stripes? He had but to lean off to baulk her rage.

We are not going to justify his conduct, we but explain his motives, some of them at least, for all could not be comprehended even by himself. His nerves were strung to the utmost pitch of tension; he was past the province of reason, and could listen only to the dictates of instinct, which, in this case suggested the right conclusion for his interests. The daughter he had offended past hope of forgiveness, the mother he had equally obliged. Were he now to thwart the latter's vengeance, he should probably lose both while terminating an unspeakable gratification mental and physical, the result not of his contrivance, but of Flora's naughtiness. Whipped she would be in any case; if modesty were outraged by the presence of a male, was that his fault? When cool he had made an honest effort to prevent; it failed, and having undertaken the duties of a hired tutor, he obeyed orders, as he was bound to do. The sin, if sin it were, was already perpetrated, and prudence pointed out the propriety of suffering the chastisement to proceed till the younger tarmagent was tamed by a discipline the severity of which her vigorous physique enabled her to bear. In fine, reason or no reason, so it was. Mack flogged, as only woman flogs, and he held on like grim death.

As a rule, women do not readily resort to rods. Some are too tender-hearted, others too chaste or too timid — but — their scruples overcome and vengeance safe, they know no measure in the cruel sport that, under the name of duty, gives the rein to passion and gratifies two lusts at every lunge. On the principle of "He's a 'oss, he *must go*" they act, and "backs" being broad and birches made to whip, *they whip indeed.*

Not till the last twig was shred from the voluminous rod did her arm cease to smite, or his to hold. "Call me liar again, if

you *dare!*   To your chamber, miss, and stay there till I let you
out."

Distracted, speechless, utterly subdued, Flo. shuffles off, her
pants about her heels, her blushes hid.

"Stop! button up before you go, and leave the shawl."

Virtue of birch! both mandates are obeyed.   The daughter
passes out, the mother follows her!   De Lancey's pulses pause
in dread lest she too vanish through the opened door. —

Not so. —

With a ha! ha! at her departed rival, she bangs it too, and
bolts it on the inside.

> "Sweets to the sweet," the fair Ophelia said,
> Or some one said it of her being dead.
> Sweet is revenge, still sweeter, if you please,
> To Mack to make a chieftain on her knees.

In the September of the following year, De Lancey being
then at the antipodes, castle and cabin at Glencabra were en
fête, the pipes skirled up, and thundering guns announced

"THE WANTED HEIR."

PEN PICTURES.

No. VII.

THE CUPID CORRECTORS.

AUNT Eleanor, in bodice and chemise
And *moiré* skirt, holds Willie on her knees;
The lecture ended, and the way made plain,
With ample room to "cut and come again."
She, seated on a stool, her hand on high,
Prepares the birchen argument to try.
So fair the boy, so beautiful the maid,
No grim scholastic image is conveyed;
You see a Venus, stript for the assault,
Correcting Cupid for some amorous fault.
Through the stained oriel the checquered light
Bathes the broad bosom, and—the other sight;
Her jewelled fingers brandishing the spray
Perhaps in punishment, perhaps in play.
He, willing to prolong the pleasing pain,
Stifles his sobs and only kicks amain.
That he *quite* likes it, scarcely can be told,
His tear-fraught eyes laugh through a shower of gold.
Pallid at first, she shrinks from every touch
And longs to ask him if it hurt too much.
As flick on flick *phisp-phisping* follows suit,
An instinct tells her *why* the boy is mute.
Instant the blood revisits cheek and lip,
She feels the fascination of the whip:

A rosebud rising o'er the bodice brim
Denotes the livelier action of the limb;
Cut follows cut *crescendo*, with a — "There,
Take *that!* and *that!* and *that!* Sir, if you dare!"
"*Woah!* wait a bit" — she lowers in a trice —
"*O Aunt! go on, don't mind me, it's so nice!*"
"*Nice!* naughty boy, I'm doing this to hurt."
"Whip, then, but wait till I pull up the skirt."
"Fie, sir! leave that." "I won't." — She does not curse,
But merely tells him that he'll get it worse,
Then opens wider by a sidelong lurch
To double the infliction of the birch.
Their mutual madness mounts with slash and shove,
The rub responding to the rasp above,
Till the whipt wolf retreats before the dove,
And Castigation culminates in Love.

THE BEAUTIFUL HERMAPHRODITE.

A Tale in Four Chapters.

CHAPTER I.

THE FIRST BIAS — CHILDHOOD OF WILLIE DAVENPORT.

THE careless world walk daily over secrets of the rarest nature, and buried histories whose dim grandeur excite awe in the soul of the palæontologist. So likewise in the moral world there are histories startling as secret; they exist, though in the majority of cases quite natural causes conspire to keep them beneath the surface. Of such recondite transactions England is obviously the frequent scene; that country being rich at once in material wealth — the creator of marvels, and in the eccentricities of its freeborn denizens. What the sudden acquisition and boundless command of money can tempt certain characters to achieve, may be gathered — by the *far*-seeing — from a perusal of the following narrative : —

Major Davenport was a gallant soldier in the service of the umquhile Honorable East India Company. Though highly connected, he had little to trust to but his good sword, which perhaps might have carved for him the road to distinction, were it not that in storming an obscure hill-fort, he was unluckily floored by a pot shot from the matchlock of a Beeloochee. There was no widow to weep his loss, for his wife had died in giving birth to their only son. And thus, at the early age of four years, was Willie Davenport thrown, almost penniless, on the cold charity of a heartless world. This is the conventional phrase, we know; but the world is not quite so bad as it is painted by scamps, who, having ruined themselves and their families, perhaps by vice or prodigality, expect to be treated by it to the fatted calf for their pains.

Certainly, kindness the most lavish was showered on the little orphan. His grandfather, Sir Horace Davenport, had been on indifferent terms with his son, and up to the date of the Major's death was scarce aware of the existence of our hero. Now, he withdrew the child from the care of a distant connexion of the family; and finding him to resemble in features the boy whom at the same age he had tenderly loved, admitted him at once to his home and his affections. He could not do much for him in the way of worldly goods, for his elbows were dreadfully worn, and he so improvident that the best tailoring of Fortune could scarcely mend them. Still the old baronet claimed all regards by his air of hereditary dignity, coupled with a naturally fine physique; stout of heart, large of limb, but not inelegant, with cheeks like winter apples, smooth shaven chin, and curls of frosted silver; a fine specimen of the "Old English Gentlemen," a species of the genus homo likely, since the admission of universal suffrage, to become extinct as the dodo or the platypus.

All Sir Horace Davenport's children were now dead or married, with the exception of his youngest daughter, Eleanor, who kept house for him. That she remained a spinster at the mature age of thirty, proved that our friend "the world" can be heartless in its way, for a golden eye-glass would have discovered in her abundant charms of person; and instead of resenting the world's indifference, she was on the best of terms with it, and ready to extend to all the blessings of a kindly heart and cheerful temper.

Eleanor Davenport would have opened her arms to any orphan, and pressed it to her loving bosom, even though ugly and uninteresting; her keen sense of the beautiful, however, was not destined to any shock of a disagreeable kind at sight of her nephew, Willie. In presenting his portrait we must observe that it is sketched rather prospectively with reference to what he afterwards became, for as yet time had not ripened and intensified the rare attributes of the infant.

Our Willie was in all respects a "lusus naturæ." When that prolific dame, Nature, does quit the beaten tract, she is capable of wild anomalies. In the present instance her ladyship's frolic mood displayed itself in change and combination. She had invested the sex and many qualities of the man in the form and soul of a woman. Not only were there the usual elements of female beauty, alabaster skin, pink cheeks, azure eyes, and rich silky curls; but, stranger still, there were the rounded limbs and breadth of pelvis proper to all Eve's representatives. If the breasts were less developed, and destitute of the lacteal apparatus, they were yet plump, smooth, and fair to look on. As to the rest, Aunt Eleanor took the earliest opportunity to convince herself of Nature's intentions as to the garb in which the beautiful infant should be arrayed; and after experience proved that, however strange the "mise ensemble," her handiwork had not been fashioned negligently.

We shall pass lightly over the opening of our hero's life, singling out only two epochal days that shaped his destiny.

As a boy, his education was directed chiefly by Aunt Eleanor, herself a clever and accomplished scholar, aided by a private tutor when her classical repertory was exhausted. In his eighteenth year his grandfather died, and the young Sir William passed to the University of Oxford. There, as a matter of course, he was laughed at for his effeminate appearance; but his singular beauty and good temper soon disarmed the quizzers. It was remarked, too, that he was not deficient in strength or pluck. He could pull a fair oar, and was unrivalled as a light weight rider. Too poor to keep horses himself, they were thrust on him by his admiring friends, for whom he won more than one steeplechase by a combination of skill and daring. There, as elsewhere, he was beloved by all.

We must now return for a brief space to the days of Willie's blissful childhood, for a happy one it was. Exquisitely sensible to the beauties of nature, these were still further enhanced by

the constant presence of visions, half classical, half epicurian.
For him every brake had its dryad, and beneath the streams his
dreamy eye could detect the undraped forms of nixies of un-
earthly loveliness.   An extract from some simple verses in
which he afterwards endeavored to recall these images will explain, better than any words of ours, his then feelings.

> When sweet May's balmy breath was by,
>   On violet bank extended,
> I'd watch the clear blue vault of sky
>   While dreamy thoughts were blended.
>
> Then, as each soft white fleecy cloud
>   Passed o'er the azure plain,
> Within its breast some wizard proud
>   In fancy I have lain.
>
> Oft would I wander out whene'er
>   To twilight night succeeded,
> Regardless of the chilly air,
>   The earned rebuke unheeded.
>
> The wonders of the night, arrayed
>   In jewel'd garb, were solved by me,
> For quickly might I call to aid
>   Romance's sweet philosophy.
>
> Then have I thought some angel kind
>   Night's sombre veil had riven,
> That here and there man's eye might find
>   The lustre light of heaven.
>
> Each orb that twinkled 'mid the swarm
>   Of countless spangles near it,
> Was darkened by the passing form
>   Of some celestial Spirit.

That a child so imaginative and so exquisitely pretty should
be loved by the warm-hearted Eleanor, was a matter of course.
To say that he returned that love would scarce be sufficient:

she was everything to him; all his nymphs and naiads assumed her voluptuous form. If she were reading, or her attention otherwise occupied, he would fix his deep blue eye on her, and his young heart would flutter with vague forbodings, in which it almost appeared as if the passions of the man were tempered by the tender love of woman.

This may seem strange — does not the most superficial observer perceive at times that strange thoughts are passing through the minds of intellectual children? These thoughts are unrecorded and forgotten ; nevertheless, the pencil of passion, whose characters are so legible on the broad canvas of mature life, writes with the reverse in miniature on the heart of childhood.

It is often alleged that the child's happiness is overrated, that its small sorrows are as keenly felt as its joys, and that the griefs preponderate. It may be so where sensitive natures are chilled by neglect or harshness. But such was not the case with Willie Davenport; so surrounded was he by an atmosphere of love he obeyed his kind mistress through impulse, and if he erred, it was because he was swayed rather by the hope than the fear of chastisement.

And this brings us to the first epochal day.

CHAPTER II.

"Dulces Amaryllidis Iræ" — Gentle Correction by Aunt Eleanor.

Willie had his faults; what man or woman has not, whose history is worth recording? Though rarely sulky, he is petulant, and his inattention to all save his aunt's orders has more than once called forth a growl from irascible Sir Horace. To-day he is more than usually troublesome, and in bounding from the breakfast table trips and tumbles over the gouty foot of his grandfather; seeing the uplifted crutch, he darts through the open window, and is off to the woods to spend the day with his loved nymphs and nixies.

When the shades of evening approach, Willie returns somewhat crest-fallen. Slipping in through a back entrance, he is encountered by his aunt's maid Charlotte, an aggravating puss not many years older than himself, who always assumed airs of authority.

"So! here you are at last, you naughty boy. What 'ave you been a doin' hov? The old gent 'as been a blowin' hup Miss Heleanor as never was. But you was to go to her directly you come in, — and whisper, my beauty, there 's a rod in pickle for you; leastways I see her cutting something sharp in the shrubbery. Aha! *Visp! Visp!*"

The boy stops and trembles, but blushes instead of turning pale. A vague presentiment agitates him; he will see his beautiful preceptress in a new light, like Juno robed in awful majesty.

Charlotte follows up the passage; when he goes in she applies her eye to the keyhole, her gown-tail sticking out over a red petticoat, her cheeks as red; what she sees there does not tend to cool them. But we will rather view the scene with the boy's romantic eyes.

He enters very softly. It is a large old-fashioned apartment, lighted by gothic windows of plain and stained glass, which form the walls of two eliptical recesses. In one of them Aunt Eleanor is standing. She is half way through her dinner toilet. Her skirt is of rich Irish poplin, the body to match is yet lying on a chair, and the slanting rays, chequered by foliage and stained glass, bathe her bare neck and arms in green and amber light, and glint from the jewels on her fingers. She looks pale and sorrowful; you would say she was the culprit, not the avenger. On a round table in the recess lie birch branches, twine, and scissors. But no grim scholastic rod is there, only three slender twigs bound loosely with a narrow blue ribbon; such a weapon as Venus might select to chastise Cupid withal.

-She is aware of the boy's presence, and endeavors to call up a stern look; the effort fails, her eyes fill with tears.

"O Willie! why will you drive me to this? I warned you not to vex your grandfather; now he threatens to send you away altogether. You promised you would attend to your lessons, and you spend the whole day idling out of doors. Kind words are of no avail; now cruel stripes must teach you the necessity of obedience."

As with pathetic tones she thus adjures him, making at the same time the necessary preparations for punishment, Willie maintains unbroken silence. He would fain be reconciled, but to utter a word might cause her to relent, and oh! it is so delicious to find himself naked beneath *her eye*, her soft hand above, and the rough silk below him! Soon the tingling sensation in his rear and the motion it imparts to his limbs, awake a new sensuous pleasure he had dreamt of indeed, but never experienced in the flesh till now.

Meanwhile how different are the feelings of Aunt Eleanor! After a few lashes of the tiny scourge, she becomes alarmed at his silence; has terror stopped his utterance?

Aunt E. "Speak, Willie! have I hurt you too much?"

Willie. "Oh! pray, pray, Aunt, go on. It's so pleasant!"

Aunt E. "Pleasant, child! I mean this for punishment."

Willie. "I know you do, and I deserve it well; but that little thing only tickles me."

Here is an astounding revelation. This will never do; to make punishment a pleasure were to destroy all discipline.

Aunt E. "Go, sir, and stand with your face in the corner. I will let you know presently what whipping is."

She now does what she should have done at first, namely, ties together a smart serviceable rod from the materials on the table. This time she does not place the culprit on her lap, but stretches him face downwards on the bed, tucks in his shirt, and takes his trousers off altogether.

Par parenthése, we beg the discerning reader to remember that Lotty's eye meanwhile is fastened to the door; we beg him

further to notice a concatenation of events similar in result to
that brought about by the missing nail in the horse's shoe.
— *e. g.*

Had Willie not left a piece of plamb cake in his aunt's cup-
board, the mice had not been so lively.

Had her rest been undisturbed, Miss Davenport would not
have ordered the position of her bed to be changed.

Had the bed been in the old corner, Lotty would not have
seen — that which she never saw before.

Had she not seen —

"Mais chacun — et chacune à son tour."

Stepping well back to the left and rear, and bidding him lie
still, Aunt Eleanor then lays on three or four raspers in succession, with the full force of her fair arm unimpeded by drapery.
Willie's limbs quiver, he clutches the bed clothes convulsively,
but as yet makes no sign of deprecation or surrender.

She pauses in wonder: the strange enthusiasm of the beautiful boy passes in an electric current from his body to her's,
making her taste for the first time that most indefinable fruit
of the tree of knowledge — the pleasure of whipping.

When women taste this, they whip in earnest.

Her arm being powerful and the rod large, the latter soon
whistled through the air and flopped into the flesh with a business like and scholastic twang, changing the alabaster skin to
intense vermillion.

Not many of these real cuts had fallen, when Willie with a
cry tumbled on one knee upon the floor, and turning to his aunt
with clasped hands and streaming eyes, implored her mercy.

The spectacle was a moving one ; for a moment she gazed in
speechless remorse, then snatching the repentant sinner to her
breast, sealed his pardon with a thousand kisses.

This emotional scene was beheld through the keyhole by
Miss Lobkins, whose line of sight brought Willie's profile between her eye and the near bedpost.

Fort bein, ma grosse fille,
Ta derrière en cotillon est bein bombèe —
Viendra l'accu*la*de sans jupes.
Ce n'est pour rien qu'on assiste aux scènes *peign*euses.
Nous verrons !

CHAPTER III.

"CÆSA FLAGRO EST PUEILLA" — HOW WILLIE LEARNED HIS VIR-
GIL — WAS N'T IT NICE — HE THINKS CHARLOTTE MIGHT SHOW
HIM A BETTER WAY — THE LESSON INTERRUPTED — THE CON-
SEQUENCE.

THE next morning Aunt Eleanor and Willie sat lovingly as
ever at a tête-à-tête breakfast. Sir Horace had been stopping
the last night at a county town, some ten miles distant, to con-
sult more conveniently his medical adviser touching the pro-
tracted visitation of gout. Aunt Eleanor is to meet him to-day,
do some shopping, and accompany him home.

"May I go with you, Aunt ? "

"No, Willie, dear, it may not be. Remember how you wast-
ed yesterday. You have not looked at your Virgil yet, and to-
morrow your tutor will be here to examine you."

Willie groans as he thinks over the prosy dialogue of Tityrus
and Melibœus; but feeling the justice of her remonstrance, he
hands his aunt cheerfully into the carriage, and betakes himself
to his task with all the patience compatible with his mercurial
temperament.

When birds twitter, bees hum, and summer air comes laden
with perfume, how horrid is the sight of a dog-eared dictionary !
It disgusts the quick scholar and bewilders the slow. A French-
man once set a youth of the latter order some easy sentences of
English to be rendered into his (Monsieur's) own language : —

"I have lost my book."   "I have found my pen."
"J' ai perdé mon livre."   "J' ai établé mon plume."

"Etabli ! — cré mon ! Vere you find zat, sare ? "

Dunderhead points to English column Fo — To found, éta-
blir, v. a., 2nd conj.

Willie looked with intense disgust at his Entick. — "Nos
dulcia linquimus arva" — I can't find dulcia — plural perhaps,
dulce domum means sweet home. Is that Charlotte's voice
singing in the laundry? She chuckled yesterday, and looked
as if she'd like to see me whipped. Did n't care if she did.
Heigh-ho! how delicious it was — at first, it hurt too much on
the bed. That Charlotte is up to so many dodges perhaps she
could show me another way; there must be one.

When Miss Davenport reached the third milestone on her
way to town, the driver, a man of few words, got down, examined the horse's off-leg, remounted the box, and turned to the
right about.

"Where are you going to, Thomas?"

"Home; horse lame."

"And Sir Horace, how is he to get back?"

"Night train."

The horse was valuable, the groom despotic; so, with a sigh
to the abandoned bonnets, Eleanor resigned herself to her fate.

The house was built in the old style; you mounted to the
hall door by a flight of steps, and the windows of the basement,
half the size of the upper ones, were flush with the ground. As
the carriage passed by, Aunt Eleanor, looking into one of the
nether windows, thought she could descry the head of her beloved Willie bobbing up and down.

There was nothing very wonderful in that; a head presup-
poses a body attached, the non-appearance of which in this
case was accounted for by the laws of optics. But if, as is as-
serted, a hat or bonnet long worn assumes a certain likeness to
the wearer, the living head, though the features be unseen, may
well have a character of its own. Aunt Eleanor's suspicions
were aroused.

"What *can* that boy be doing in the laundry?"

The hall-door was open, she glided down stairs, and turning
the handle noiselessly, beheld the following tableau : —

A petticoat vanishing through the opposite door; a deal table in the centre, with flannel and flat irons; behind it "sweet Willie," blushing from head to tail, and assuming momently a more crest-fallen aspect under her stony glare.

"Button up!" She hissed out the words, and scarce allowing time for the act, dragged him up the stairs, opened a closet at the landing, pushed him in and turned the key.

Fierce as her anger was, but small measure of it was directed against him.

"That wicked wretch! Only a few months ago in my Sunday school, and now what has she taught the child! out she shall pack without a character, and her mother shall know the reason why. But first for Willie. Papa must not hear of this. I must punish the boy before he comes back — at once — now."

Now was indeed the best time for a visit to the shrubbery, the coast could scarce be clearer. The fat cook never left the lower regions, Charlotte would keep out of the way of course, and Thomas the taciturn, had his horse to mind.

To the sportsman, the stock and lock of his Purdy in September — to the maiden, her first ball-dress — are suggestive; but scarcely so much so as the first tying of the rod. There are born rodmakers, of whom Aunt Eleanor, all unconsciously to herself, was one. Carefully she waxed the proper length of twine, selected and trimmed the longest stems, combining them so as to equipoise the handle with the budding honors of the top, and secure the strength and elasticity of the blow. As she snipped off the last bit of cord with the scissors, she shook the rod in the air. It was a perfect gem of art, and would have whipped of itself in the veriest tyro's hand.

How it must hurt! she thought; I have a mind to try. But hush! Who can that be knocking at the door?

She hid the rod and opened. Without stood Charlotte, her apron at her eyes, beseeching to be heard.

"You wicked, wicked girl, how dare you present yourself before me, after what has occurred? Go, till I send for you."

But Charlotte pressed in. "Hear me, Miss, for pity's sake;

it wern't my fault. I declare to gracious goodness I never
dreamt of harm no more than if it had been a woman or a babe.
I 'll tell you the blessed truth word for word. I was a thinking
of Master Willie, which I knew you whip the pretty creature,
leastways I guessed, because I see you from the tool-house
cutting the rod. Just then he cum in looking that sarcy, I
could n't help asking him how he felt in his behind. He an-
swers sharp as a needle, it only hurted him in one place, which
he 'd show me where. I was stooping on the table, Miss, iron-
ing your chemise, and ere ever I was hup to his tricks, he had
his 'and on my neck, and ―― O ! Miss, he 's as strong as any
man, is that boy."

"A likely story, indeed, that a child like that could do it, if
you did not show him how ! Pack up your things and leave
this at once. To-morrow I shall go to the village, pay your wages
to Mrs. Dobkins, and let her know the reason why I turned
you off."

Now, this was what Charlotte most dreaded. Mrs. Lobkins,
her mother, was a sour-visaged, strong-minded methodist, who,
having few weaknesses of her own to recall, had no mercy on
her children's faults, and never spared the correction by King
Solomon enjoined. She enlarged even on the text, the "rod"
in her Darconian code being mere child's play. Over the man-
tlepiece she kept in terrorem three souple bamboo canes lashed
together at one end ; with these, having first let down their
smocks and tied their hands to the bed-post, she would belabor
the backs of Lotty or her sisters till the blood ran down.

When the maiden thought what she would get for her late
lapse and loss of place, it curdled the marrow in her bones.

"O Miss Healeanor ! you that was halways so good and kind.
I know I must go, but you said as I was n't bright at my needle.
Let mother think it 's for that. She 'd kill me if she knew the
truth."

"And do you imagine I am going to let wickedness like yours
be concealed to save you from a beating ? Begone, and pack
your things."

"Mercy, Miss Heleanor! Punish me yourself the way you would master Willie; only worse, for I did n't ought to 'ave let 'im hin."

Miss Davenport paused. Like the tigress she had been robbed of her whelp, and like her had tasted blood. Here was the creature that had revelled in the embraces she dared not permit herself, at her mercy — and the rod at hand.

"Charlotte Lobkins," she said solemnly, "what you ask is no light thing. By one or the other you must and shall be punished as your crime deserves. I know the kind of beatings you get at home, and they are scarcely too bad for the present act. If I were to intercede for you with your mother, and promise to take you back a month hence when Master Davenport goes to school, — if I were, I say, to do all this, would you allow your bottom to be whipped with a birch rod, without disturbing the house with your cries?"

"And you won't tell Mother what I done?"

"Not if you obey my orders now."

"Oh! bless you, Miss, for that. Don't fear my crying for the rod; only try. Has for horders, you shan't 'ave no horders to give."

Miss Lubkins then went to the drawer, asked leave to use some tape, which she cut in equal lengths, and fastened to the front legs of a couch that lay crossways at the end of the bed; this she wheeled in the same direction with it, and placed a hassock at the foot. In a minute more she stood in her smock, coarse but clean, surrounded by a pile of clothes, her half laced stays still on, struggling with the broad back and shoulders.

Now, Charlotte's flesh was plump and fair, where not exposed; her hair was of a rich reddish brown, her eyes were hazel, her cheeks and lips vermillion. In short, barring a saucy cock of the nose, which some thought became her, Miss C. Lobkins claimed to be, and was a pretty girl. We seize this moment to paint her picture, because it is a fair one, she being little indebted now to meretricious ornament. And if you do not like her as she is, you must at least admire her pluck,

though that was rather the result of ignorance. As she tucked
the shift around her waist she smiled, and the roses in her
cheek deepened instead of paling. From the gray stays and
its margin of white the haunches stood out, massive, round and
firm, like blocks of granite; not a muscle quivered, as in more
experienced rears it would have done in such predicament. Her
sturdy thighs seemed lined with plates of steel, her feet and
ankles were incased in lace-up boots, and over the too substantial calves the hose were tightly drawn, their color red to match
with the discarded petticoat.

"Of two evils choose the least." Turning her back respect-
fully to her mistress, Lotty made fig-leaves of her hands, and
stood at the couch-foot waiting the advent of the rod. When it
appeared she eyed the graceful weapon with a queer and quaint
expression.

"Wait a bit, Miss, please." — (Is Lotty going to cave in?)

"'Adn't I best tuck this aneath the stays, afear it cum down
and my 'ands tied?'"

This she did with a reckless disregard of even the legitimate
shelter which the last garment might have afforded to the lower
part of her person; then kneeling well into the centre of the
hassock, she stooped till her elbows rested on the couch, and
tendered her wrists, which Miss Davenport secured by a series
of tight-drawn knots from which the scissors only could release
them.

Lotty Lobkins, though well versed in the coarser strategy of
the stick, never having been at other than a Sunday school, had
no conception of the subtleties of birching; else assuredly she
had not acted thus rashly. Never was fix more awkward than
that in which her own ministry had helped to place her. Her
strong hands, struggle as she might, were now powerless; the
couch was low; the hassock, too broad and cumbrous to be
kicked aside, raised her knees to near the level of her head,
thereby presenting the broad end fully "bombed" to meet the
birch, and exposing to its vengeance that for the criminal in-
dulgence of which she was about to suffer.

Would you like to know how many, and what sort of skelps the young sinner got for this her first faux-pas?   Listen, then, and count them.

Whisp! Whisp! Whisp!

[The hand not being yet in, the first taste produces only a grunt, half digestive, half defiant.]

Whisp! Whisp! Whisp! Whisp! Whisp! Whisp!

[The taste is decidedly unpalatable, witness heaving stomach, smothered groans, and squealing.]

Whisp! Whisp! Whisp! Whisp! Whisp! Whisp!

"*Blast it, Miss Heleanor!   Leave horrrf, or I shall 'oller!*"
"If you do, I'll tell your mother.   Put your foot down."

Whisp! Whisp! Whisp! Whisp! Whisp! Whisp!

[Only gurglings now, the face being buried in the sofa cushion.]

Whisp! Whisp!   Flick, flick, flick!!!

[The whisps delivered at full range ; the flicks perpendicular at close quarters.]

The striker steps back once more, and viewing with regret the mutilated condition of the weapon, concenters her fury in a circling

SLASH!

that snaps the rod across, and finishes the discipline.

Lotty, cut loose, staggers to the water bottle, and by a gulp of its contents, prevents herself from fainting.

We doubt if henceforward she will not prefer even the triple bamboo.

Yet, with a heroism the more admirable that there are none to witness it, the plucky girl while resuming her attire, endeavors to appear indifferent.

Nenni, ma chère, the crimson stains on the chemise, the blubbered cheeks and choking sobs too plainly tell of anguish.

The exercise above described afforded such relief to the outraged virtue of Miss Davenport that the male culprit was set free at once, but ordered for punishment at six, a. m., next day.

At the hour prescribed, Willie knocked at his aunt's door, and receiving no reply, entered, bolted it behind him, and stealing to the bed-side, found her immersed in slumber, how profound he was too innocent to test in the right way, Charlotte's lesson having been given under dissimilar circumstances. She lay on the broad of her back, the bed-clothes on account of the heat half flung off, her chestnut curls strewing the pillow. The vermillion lips, a little apart, were wreathed into a smile ill becoming the stern purpose of the preceptress. Can she be really asleep — her eyelids seem to see him?

"Aunt, it's six o'clock. Please get up and whip me."

No response.

Slipping his hands beneath her night dress, he tickles her bosom lightly to awaken her.

"Naughty boy, I told you what I'd do."

She rose in seeming wrath, went to the wardrobe, and drew forth — even the old Cupid correctors. These she laid upon the bed, undid the brace buttons, and opened the front of his Russia ducks. Unwilling to expose him in the position in which he then stood, she did not suffer the continuations to descend more than a few inches; without removing the sustaining hand, she lectured him for some time in guarded terms such as the nature of his offence required. The lecture ended, she let fall the ducks, and led him, shuffling but nothing loath, to the stool where he had first suffered, on which she seated herself, robed only in — "the dress you wear, my Nora Creina." She now removed the ducks altogether, and made other necessary preparations in the liberal style suggested the previous day by Lotty.

This she did, turning the boy slowly and deliberately round the while, stern necessity obliging her now to expose without reference to position. Seizing her victim by the waist and leg, she hoisted him on to the altar of her lap, arranging his position there by sundry pulls and pushes.

Up to this, Willie had remained passive in her hands, or if he moved, only doing so in furtherance of her wishes.   But —

After a few flicks and flings, there ensued a duel between the pair, conducted, we regret to say, by both parties in a manner so improper, our modesty is compelled to refer the reader for a mitigated description thereof to the Pen Picture, wherein the leading features of both "affairs" are amalgamated.

> The *Painter* choosing, be it understood,
> To take her in a mild or madder mood.

Stop though — Was that a fair allotment of punishment? Hardly so.

But Lotty must learn the lesson of her sex — how much worse it is to suffer than to do.

CHAPTER IV.

A SHORT ONE, AND FULL OF ——— NO MATTER.

The thief said: — "The lock of the carpet-bag always make his knife laugh."

So it is with the writer and reader of a tale. All the author's deepest dodges and quaintest mystifications, which serve to keep the fancy of the conscientious reader on the stretch, cannot prevent the impatient one from jumping at once to the conclusion.

Here the carpet-bag laughs at the thief.

How our beautiful Hermaphrodite won the heart of a crusty millionaire, who dying soon after, left him countless treasures, how he then assumed the garb most suited to his appearance and designs, and passed, virile but unprolific, through a boarding-school of delighted fledglings, and from thence into the boudoirs of the fairest of the land ——

These secrets are contained in our carpet-bag; and let any thief of a reader pick them if he can.

End of The Beautiful Hermaphrodite.

PEN PICTURES.

No. VIII.

"WHICH OF YOU TWO DID THAT?"

THE ALARM—(UNSEEN.)

WHILE on her path to-ward the bath,
  In cap, chemise, and skirt,
Ma hears the row, and vows a vow
  Her powers to exert.
The button holds the flannel's folds,
  She tries it with a shove,
Then drops adrift the slipping shift
  That hampers her above.
She makes a bound, but turns her round
  To seek a certain key,
With what design you may divine,
  Then up the stairs strides she.

THE QUESTION — (SEEN.)

"Which of you two the mirror threw?"
  Ma asks with venom'd grin.
The crystal smashed, the girls abashed,
  Young Harry peeping in.
But Agnes' eye mounts proud and high,
  She *won't* be whipped; in fact
While Pussy pale concocts a tale,
  Her saucy sister's smack'd.
"No right, quotha? You *won't*,—ha! ha!
  Take *that* to tame your pride,
And since you dare dispute, prepare
  By menials to be tried.
I'll ring the bell for Mrs. Fell,
  For Prance and Pinner."—"Stay,
Don't ring, I'll go." "You'd better so,
  Strip then and lead the way."
But Harry's door is right before,
  If here she strip, he'll see.
With sulky bend she lifts the end—
  No higher than the knee.
"Up with you shift this instant!"— Swift
  She swings aloft the train,
With staying hand on breeches' band,
  She shuffles past the pane
Where Harry's eyes, and yours likewise,
  Squint after her in vain.
And here let a suggestive light be shed
On patient Pussy weeping by her bed.

HOMEWARD BOUND.

FORECAST AND CAUTION.

Can you not give us something from a source
    Other and brighter than the tear-fraught Rod?
We gave a promise to be good perforce ——
    Still, if the captious critic will but nod
Like Homer, who,* asleep was good of course,
    We'll try; the exception shall at least be odd:
The ocean billows, as they homeward roll
In smooth monotony, shall raise the *sole*.

* Aliquando etiam bonus dormitat Homerus. — HORACE.

PEN PICTURES.

No. IX.

PURSUIT OF KNOWLEDGE UNDER DIFFICULTIES.

I.

THE riddle that the wise man readeth not
   Is often simple as Columbus' eggs.
The Captain, rising on his cabin cot,
   Ponders the problem of the Lifted Legs,
The azure garters, and the snowy screen
With just a peep of pretty pink between,
And if it were not for the wicker gate,
The Peri Paradise might enter straight.

II.

An odd fish she must look above the deck,
   Sed piscis desinit in mulierem;
To prove if fish or flesh without a check,
   Other than physical, were worth a gem——
A gem— Gadso! the ring, the ring's the mean
With which to catch the conscience of the quean;
Dropt in a purse between the leg and hose
'T will silence all the scruples that oppose.

III.

How vast the volume, and how taut the strain!
   The creaseless linen almost threatens rents;
'T would puzzle even a Colenso's brain
   To calculate the cubical contents.

Still, like the grapes above the longing fox,
The double disc is lifted by the box.
The Captain eyes the space from deck to shoe,
And asks himself again what shall he do.

IV.

Shall the fix'd mountain come to Me-ho-mèt?
  Or must the prophet to the mountain rise?
The first would light on the proceedings let,
  To do the second, passes power of thighs;
However willing she to make it slack,
The baffling boards would lay him on his back.
A fair solution will no doubt be found,
For hers is *Love Afloat*, and he is *Homeward Bound*.

HOMEWARD BOUND ; OR, LOVE AFLOAT.

A Tale in One Chapter.

CONTENTS.

A LEARNED SHIP'S COOK — BARRACK BEAUTIES — THE GIG IMPOS-
TOR — THE TALISMAN — "FURENS QUID FÆMINA."

THE ocean will ever have its romance, though even that of
late is wofully minished. In these go-a-head days you step
a-board a P. and O. steamer wrapped in muffles and mackin-
tosh, and ere you have time to get at your jeans, find yourself
sweltering off the Spanish coast. Poetry still clung round the
Overland Route; where is now the desert caravan with its
Arab guard and social joltings ? Vanished into the mirage before the shriek of the all-pervading steam engine.

But I speak of old days, good or bad as the reader pleases,
when a voyage was a voyage, not a succession of ferry-boats;
when, as you mounted the deck of a heavy laden merchantman,
you looked curiously on its living freight, crew inclusive, knowing that whatever their social qualities, pleasant or the reverse,
they, and they only, would be your companions for months to
come.

On this particular voyage, with full details of which I shall
not weary your patience, there was apparently as little scope
for adventure as might well be. The only male passenger was
your humble servant, and of the softer sex there were but two
quasi ladies, of whom anon. The skipper was a young man little older than myself, a pleasant, genial fellow, who could command his men without assuming the airs of a martinet. We

fraternised at once, and he did his best to make things pleasant; no very easy task had I been a Sybarite, for the vessel, designed chiefly for cargo, was ill found in luxuries, and we were
soon reduced to the ship's larder of potted meats and salt junk.

> " I 'll not leab dee, dou lone'un,
>   To pine on de stem,"

said Sambo the black cook, as he compassionately cut the throat
of the last hen, about the third week of the voyage.

You stare. A cook, and a black one, quote the melodies ! So
it was, however. Our Soyer was an original, and a born poet.
Nor was Sambo's talents confined to poetry alone, for he dabbled
a little in metaphysics, astronomy, and divers others abstruse
subjects. Heaven knows where he had been "half baptised,"
but the terms of science at least were familiar to him. A little
learning is a dangerous thing, and the smattering with which
Sambo was imbued, did not tend to the diminution of his natural arrogance. I think I must treat you to one of his harangues,
jotted down verbatim one moonlight night, as we smoked our
pipes perdus under the lee of the galley.

Sambo loquiter.

"Come here, you boy Jim. Golly ! what for him allus run —
run — run ? 'Tan' till, I tell 'ee; my feelin' must ab vent. Now
I read page from um hebbenly book. Berry hard book dat,
Jim, but nebber fear ; 'pose you no sabby tink I say — ax question agin; den *revolve upon um's axes*, Hi! hi! hi! Now look,
see dat round yaller light dat shine there up in um hebbens.
Kye! what you tink make dat ? "

"Why the moon, to be sure."

"Ho! you darn ignoran' white boy ! Not dat him so white
neider. Pshaugh! no fit to touch wid de tongs. Dat not de
moonlight."

"Well, dash my wig ! (an abstertion by the way by no means
uncalled for) dash my wig if ever I heard the like o' that afore."

"No, sir; dat de light ob um sun. You tinks, cos nebber reflect, dat de sun gone dead; but sun leab um light behind, and
de sensible moon, *him* reflect it."

Here Sambo paused and gazed with rapt vision, now on the luminary, now in Jim's face, but finding no response in the wooden and dirt-grimmed features of the latter, he shook his head with intense disgust, and thus proceeded: —

"'Pose you tink too de world all flat and nebber 'tir. Hech! world more round nor orange, and allus go whirl—whirl—whirl at end of um chain, jist so as I 'pin knife wid lanyard. And reason for why all men nebber fall off—dat sir, what we call de *centipede 'traction*. But och whurra! what for talk? It plain you no comprehen' ebbery two word I 'peak. Dere! (hitting him a rap on the head) "go scour um pot and grubble like pig in um native helement!"

Allez, maintenant, M. le Cuisinier, faites places aux dames.

Mrs. Quartermaster Murphy and Mrs. Sergeantmajor Jenkins, of the ———, but that would be "telling," were sworn sisters. Any trifling discrepancy in their relative standing in the regiment had been lost sight of during the perils of a common journey, unattended by their lords, from up-country to the coast. Indeed the balance of respectability tended in favor of her of lesser rank, for honest Mary Murphy made no secret of her penchant for grog, and it was known that in camp she and the Quartermaster consumed between them seven case bottles of gin hebdomadally.

Mrs. Jenkins was a wiry, active woman, and a thorough soldier's wife. She would allow any liberties of speech, but as far as I knew to the contrary, was substantially virtuous. She liked a word of praise from the men, from the officers more, but dressed becomingly according to her station.

Not so the fair Murphy; she delighted in gaudy colors, and made liberal display of her more than budding charms of an evening. She was meant for a pretty woman, and must have been eminently such a few years earlier, ere tropical suns had stolen the roses from her cheeks, and over imbibation of barrels of Bass had caused her person to assimilate.

This lovely being soon set the eyes of affection — well, I hope on me — certainly on a small diamond I wore in a hoop of In-

dian gold on the right third finger. One night we had remained up the last of the cuddy party, and were getting confi-
dential over the biscuit and brandy-pawnee.

"Oh! Captain jewel, would you have me break me marridge
vows, and may be get into trouble on the head of it ?"

And seizing my presumptuous hand, she imprisoned it between her plump ones. In this amorous dalliance she contrived
to transfer the diamond to her own little finger.

"See then if it was n't made for it."

I pleaded it was a gage d'amour, forgetting to add that the
donor was Cheap Jack — "for a consideration."

Her lips said nothing of exchange, but like the trafficers in
Eastern bazaars, the expressive fingers indicated the value she
was willing to give for the article.

"Her parting gift," I said, "impossible."

She returned it with a sigh and an incredulous shake of the
head. And that reminds me of an apt illustration, pardon that
I interrupt you.

The son of an English baronet had been amusing himself
"more *Majorum*" in Irish country quarters. When the route
came he delivered his p.p.c.'s in person. Amongst other friends
he called on Mrs. Magennis. "And is it goin' ye are without
askin' for Matilda ?" The subaltern hoped the young lady was
well, and expressed regret at not seeing her. "Baithershin!"
said the fond parent, and this time it was the "Mither press'd
him sair." At length she put the question point blank — "Will
ye marry her ?" "My dear Madam," he replied, "nothing
would give me greater pleasure, but it would be an injustice to
Miss Matilda; I have only my pay to live on." "Ach! ye im-
posther ye, don't ye keep a gig ?"

The next day was intensely hot ; there was a breeze indeed,
before which we slipped a few knots, but it seemed to be
breathed from a furnace. I lay in shirt and sleeping drawers
on a low couch in my cabin, my head against the open port, the
door hooked back ; beside me was a bowl of nominally cold tea,
and a porous chattee of ditto water; on the floor lay Sambo's

illustrated copy of "The Melodies." It had just struck seven
bells in the forenoon, and though not "evening bells," they reminded me of "love and youth and that sweet time." My heart,
recoiling from the arid east, flew forward to greet the sparkling
streams and rosy girls at home. A noise recalled me to the
present. Looking straight before me, I was aware of a pair of
legs, unmistakeably feminine, perched seemingly in mid air between my eyes and the outer light.

Rising, I found the following explanation of the phenomenon.
The deck had been pierced to admit the passage of a windsail,
which was now under repair in the sailmaker's hands. Like
myself, Mrs. Murphy had been incommoded by the heat. She
rose in the simplest of costume, buttoned on a jacket, and shov-
ing a sea-chest and a stool beneath, mounted thereon, and thrust
her head and shoulders through the aperture. Thus she stood,
as explained, in mid air, resting her elbows on the deck, and
exchanging now and then a remark with a passing mariner. In
this there was no seeming impropriety; her bust was decorous-
ly draped, and that beneath which "passèd show," completely
blocked the opening. To do her justice, Mary was always bien
chaussée, her ankles were neat, the tight-drawn hose were of
spotless white, and the brief chemise allowed fully two-thirds
of the calf (cow?) to be visible — and tangible.

Flesh and blood could not resist the provocation. I spanned
the ankle with thumb and forefinger; it kicked, and the body
threatened to descend. Hastily withdrawing the coveted diamond from my finger, I dropped it as in a purse between the
stocking and garter, pressing it against the flesh to indicate the
nature of the talisman. The effect was magical; never did
Genie, slave of the *ring*, obey more implicitly. Thenceforth all
of Mary Murphy below the waist was at my entire disposal.
True, it was love-making under difficulties, how great I need
not say; but what will not skill and combination effect? After
a couple of laborious minutes I could say with the Peri: —

> "Joy, joy forever — my task is done,
> The gate is pass'd, and heaven is won."

When first the fair Murphy flourished her diamond-decked digit in the cabin, Mrs. Sergeantmajor said with a wink —

"My word, ma'am, before you put your finger into that, another ring had something else through it; I hope it fitted you as tight as that one."

Just then a Jack overhead struck up the thrilling capstern ditty —

> "Oh! if I had her
> Up against a ladder."

Whereupon the two ladies roared in chorus, showing that there were no secrets between them.

I must not dismiss this specimen pair without relating a story connected with them, which certainly redounds not a little to their credit as heroines.

I said that their journey from Deeza to Bombay was perilous. The distance is some hundreds of miles, and mostly through what is called the Bheel or Robbers' country. Application was consequently made to the officer commanding the station, who allowed them a small Sepoy guard for protection. For many days their course was unmolested, and such freedom from annoyance is sure, with the troops of Hindostan, unless officered by Europeans, to induce a relaxation of discipline, of which the Bheels, who had probably been tracking them for some time, were prompt to avail themselves.

Breakfast was over, and arms piled in front of the travellers' little camp. The morning's march having been one of unusual fatigue, the vital precaution of placing sentries was entirely neglected, and the havildar, after lazily warning the men for duty to be on the look-out, placed his back against a mango tree and dozed over his hubble bubble. On every side might be seen the form of Jack Sepoy stretched on the green sward, his head nestled in numerous folds of linen, in the unmolested enjoyment of "black-man's fun," which every Anglo-Indian is aware, is neither more nor less than deep sleep.

Such was the disreputable state of affairs when a shout was heard, followed by a hail-storm of arrows, and in a moment the ground was covered with Bheels who, springing from the thicket, and probably despising their inert opponents, fell at once upon a palankin which, from the information of their spies, they knew to contain the most valuable booty.

The first impulse of the guard naturally was to spring to their feet, unpile arms, and discharge them wildly into the air; but there the instinct of discipline halted. The Sepoy, who, well led, will follow his officer through the thickest fire — (I beg pardon, you know exactly what I was going to say on that subject, or if you don't, you have read precious little about India) these Sepoys, I say, seeing themselves outnumbered, and the baggage which they ought to have guarded surrounded by an impassible barrier of foes, cast one look of blank dismay at the havildar, who was already slipping on his sandals for a run.

And run they most assuredly would, had not the god of battles, and of bandboxes too, if such a one there be, inspired the soul of Mrs. Jenkins, the Sergeantmajor's wife. Concealed in a contiguous palkee, she had witnessed in mortal terpidation the first onslaught of the Bheels. Terror had prostrated the powers of her active mind; but as the ruthless work of spoliation continued, her whole soul revolted. Leather shoes and pots of bear's greese were wisped with shawls of priceless Cashmere, and thrust into the robbers' greasy cumberbunds. All this she had seen and stirred not; but when at length sacrilegious hands were about to be laid on that blue bandbox containing the chefs d'œuvre of Madame Pélerine's last consignment from Bombay — the pent volcano burst.

O Queen of heaven! she exclaimed, "my Paris caps! real Valenciennes — twenty rupees a yard — and all paid for — I'll die first."

So saying, and with the air of an enraged Pythoness, she sprung through the startled ranks of the Bheels and placed herself at the head of her wavering guard.

"Sepoys, 'tention! close your ranks; with ball cartridge prime and load — Ready — P'sent (bang! bang! bang!) Port arms — charge bayonets!"

Everything was executed according to her orders. The Sepoys, thus aroused, poured in a murderous volley, and followed it with a charge as deadly, which left eight or ten of the enemy stretched upon the field, and completely routed the remainder, who fled without casting another glance upon the much prized box, the attempt to rifle which had cost them so dear.

THE END